TROUBLE AT TEMESCAL

TROUBLE AT TEMESCAL

A WESTERN DUO

FRANK BONHAM

edited by

BILL PRONZINI

BLACK STONE PUBLISHING

© 1951 by Popular Publications, Inc. © renewed 1979 by Frank Bonham.
© 2010 by David Bonham for restored material. © 2010 by David Bonham
Foreword © 2010 by Bill Pronzini
Published in 2018 by Blackstone Publishing

Printed in the United States of America

ISBN 978-1-4708-6174-2
Fiction / Westerns
1 3 5 7 9 10 8 6 4 2

CIP data for this book is available
from the Library of Congress

Blackstone Publishing
31 Mistletoe Rd.
Ashland, OR 97520

www.BlackstonePublishing.com

CONTENTS

FOREWORD

by Bill Pronzini

During the 1940s, Frank Bonham wrote scores of novelettes and short stories for such Western and adventure pulp magazines as *Dime Western*, *Ace-High Western*, *Lariat*, *Blue Book*, and *Action Stories*. His output of short fiction substantially declined in the early 1950s, as the pulp markets dwindled and his focus shifted to longer works. "Trouble at Temescal" (*Argosy*, 11/51), was one of only six stories to appear under his byline in 1951, and his last piece of magazine fiction was published the following year. From then on he devoted himself exclusively to Western, mystery, and young adult novels.

Set in the pueblo of Los Angeles in the days following the Mexican-American War, "Trouble at Temescal" tells the tale of two entrepreneurial mustangers, Hank Ashwood and Red Wolfe, who have driven a herd of horses from New Mexico to California for resale. Their efforts to sell the animals to one of the Mexican hacendados—Dona Julia de la Torre, owner of Rancho Temescal—are hampered by a scabrous group of squatters led by Owen Pike, bent on claiming rights to her land. Racially biased ownership laws, the actions of a hot-tempered neighbor, Ramon Calder, Ashwood's growing love for Julia, and his partner's unexpected duplicity provide additional complications. As with all of Bonham's Western and historical fiction, the historical period and background are accurately and colorfully depicted, and there is excitement aplenty throughout.

A total of seventeen Western novels appeared under the Bonham byline between 1948 and 1980, outstanding among them such titles as *Snaketrack*, *Blood on the Land*, *Night Raid*, *Hardrock*, and *Logan's Choice*. (His last novel, *Eye of the Hunter*, was published posthumously in 1989.) Action, suspense, deftly developed characters, and a fine sense of time and place are the hallmarks of each of these works. *King of the Defiances* is the restored version of an original paperback novel by Frank Bonham, first published in 1956 and appearing in this form for the first time. It is the story of Big Jim Jackson, former boss of the range in the Defiance Mountains who was driven out after his twenty-year government lease expired and who intends to return to make a new fortune by logging off the best railroad-tie timber in Arizona; and of former man hunter Troy Cameron, the leader of a group of small cattle ranchers who stand in Jackson's way. Through devious means, Jackson now holds notes on the ranchers' land and plans to foreclose if the notes aren't met on time. And he has a hired crew of gun hands ready to use force against anyone who resists. With all of this power behind him, Jackson is confident he'll have little trouble once again crowning himself King Defiance. But he doesn't reckon on the determination of Cameron, a man whose fighting spirit makes him a fearsome adversary.

TROUBLE AT TEMESCAL

I

Beyond the meadow he could see a vineyard, and beyond the vineyard the huge adobe building with sheds and outer houses huddled like hawk-frightened chicks around a hen. The lacy, round heads of peppertrees made shade everywhere.

"What they call a hacienda, I reckon," Hank Ashwood said. He whittled shavings for a fire, his big, horseman's hands easy and familiar with the Green River knife stroking off the long, even curls of wood.

From the gully beside their horse camp, Red Wolfe came swinging into view with the dripping water bags bearing him down. He poured some water into the Dutch oven and began crumbling jerky into it. "We sure come to the right place, Hank. There's money in this outfit. I hear these California hacendados are crazy for a blond, whether it's a horse or a woman. I'm telling you what's the truth. We'll sell these yella horses at a hundred a head."

"I'd feel surer of it if they were blond women," Hank Ashwood said.

Chain-hobbled, the horse herd grazed tranquilly. Aside from

the need for currying, they looked good—ex-army mounts, most of them, bought cheaply in New Mexico and trailed to the pueblo of Los Angeles for resale.

Red threw a handful of dried vegetables into the kettle. He was a stretchy, middle-size man of twenty-five who could never sit easy; he had to be busy all the time. Around a horse camp it came in handy. He took a deep breath. "Smoke yonder must be the town. Real hell roarer, what I heard." The thin dusting of freckles spread across his face with a quick smile. "You know what I'm going to do with my cut of these here plugs?"

"Blow it on craps, women, and whiskey … in two days. After five months on the trail."

Hank spoke gruffly and gave the stew a stir. But he smiled a little in his whisker stubble. Red would do all right. A mite wild, maybe, but his red head was screwed on tightly enough when it counted. They had met in Santa Fe, when Hank was just out of the army and Red was on the loose from some moneymaking project or another that hadn't paid off—Hank had never learned just what. Some horse talk over a bottle of whiskey had made them friends; Red knew his way around, and Hank had some back pay and poker winnings burning in his pocket. So they became partners. They finished the bottle and shook hands and went out to look over the army mounts. Five months had brought them this far along the trail, and about as close as two men can get.

From his possible sack Red had produced a steel mirror and was looking himself over. He bared his teeth and fingered a knife scar on his cheek bone. "Buddy, I'll strike a hard bargain with the señoritas hereabouts. They'll know how Red Wolfe likes his bacon before I leave. How 'bout you? What you figuring to do with your cut?"

"I'll find something," Hank said.

When the fire was going well, the smoke seemed to release something in both of them. They stood, watching the sunset fume along the horizon, until Red noticed a covey of blackbirds strutting on the cropped grass a hundred feet away. Abruptly he drew his Colt and fired into their midst. One of them exploded into feathers as the rest scurried off.

"What the hell was that for?" Hank said.

Red grinned devilishly at the smoking pistol as he said: "Ain't you ever felt that way? So full of vinegar you could bust? Man, what are you … a gelding or something?"

Hank smiled, but he pointed out across the gullied pasture. "If the people in that castle ain't used to gringos, they'll be putting furniture in front of the doors tonight."

"They ought to be used to 'em. If they ain't, they'll know about Yankees before we leave."

A few minutes later they heard the horseman coming across the field from the buildings. It was now late dusk, and the windows of the ranch house were orange with lamplight. There were the sounds of cows lowing to be milked, of sheep, and the family sounds of chickens going to roost. The fragrance of wood smoke and food drifted past Hank Ashwood's nose. He would always think of charcoal fumes and frying chilies when he thought of Mexicans.

Red was shaving cake coffee into their cups, listening to the oncoming hoofbeats. His face gleamed with wicked expectancy.

Hank poured hot water. "Listen, kid," he said mildly, "don't forget we're in somebody else's town, now. Have your fun, but remember you're a guest."

Red snorted. "The hell you say! This is California, ain't it? And California's a state of the Union now, ain't it? We licked them Mexes for fair. They get off the sidewalks for us."

"If it comes to that. But it don't have to come to it. These people were here a couple of hundred years before us. They never made trouble. Now there's plenty of the kind of woman you're looking for, and plenty of places to raise hell, without riling up the decent folks …"

"What the hell's gone and got into you?" Red stared at him.

"Why didn't you tell me you were a preacher? Why, hellfire, man, we could have had chapel every night."

"For a fella your size that's a lot of mouth you're flapping ..."

Red came up quickly, swirling the coffee in his cup, staring with open hostility. Across the fire from him Hank got to his feet, not quite casually. "It's this way," he told the redhead. "We want some money out of these horses. We won't get it by going on the butt with our customers." His square, dark face said he was offering an explanation, nothing else.

After a moment, Red grunted. "Now, that makes sense."

They were sitting on the ground with their pie pans in their laps, eating half-cooked stew, when the horseman arrived.

He came like a flourish of trumpets. Loping his horse directly into the camp, he put it to a plowing halt on its hind legs and then, with a lift of his reins, hauled it over to the fire. Hank stared, not alarmed, just amazed. The man handled the magnificent horse like a god. He was a young Mexican with coppery skin.

He was furious. Hank was glad the Green River knife rested on his plate.

The Mexican said: *"Buenas noches, caballeros."*

"Hi, Mex," Red said. He speared a bit of meat and took it in his teeth.

The face of the Mexican worked. He was blue eyed, so Hank guessed him to be of Spanish blood. Whatever his blood, it was boiling.

Hank said gravely: *"¡A sus órdenes, amigo!"*

The courtesy tamed the man a little. He addressed his next remark to Hank. *"¿Habéis tirado una pistola?"*

"Yeah, we shot a gun," Red said.

"¿Porqué?"

"Porqué you no speak English, if you understand it?" Red demanded.

Still speaking Spanish the man said: "I understand English, but

I speak my own tongue. That is all right?"

"Sure. You talk spik. We talk English."

Hank set his plate down and stood up, wiping his knife with two fingers. "Señor," he said, "we're mustangers. We come a long way today and we're plumb glad to get here. My partner took a shot at a bird, just because he felt good. I felt the same way, but I just grinned. The shot didn't mean any more than my grin. Only you heard it."

"Yes," the Mexican said. "We did."

Red walked around, looking at the horse. "You the boss man? You look too green to boss much of anything."

He was grinning a little, but Hank knew that American humor was not Mexican humor. The Californian's anger was rising like the neck feathers of a fighting cock as he stiffly watched Red circle the horse.

"I am Ramon Calder. This is Rancho Temescal, the de la Torre Ranch. I am a neighbor of the owner."

"Who's the owner, Ray?"

"Dona Julia de la Torre."

Red gave him that brash grin. "Prob'ly call her Julie, where we come from. How old is she?"

"Old enough to hate gringos," snapped the Mexican.

Red frowned. "Maybe we ought to drop around and show this lady how lovable we are."

Hank said quickly: "Cut it out, Red. Señor Calder, all we want is pasturage for some horses until we sell them. We figured to pay our respects to the *patrón* and find out if we could leave them here."

"You figured," the Californian said, "to squat here until you could claim the land. Like the others in Pike's company."

"Pike? Who's Pike?"

Calder repeated softly: "Who is Pike!" He laughed without humor.

Red's back stiffened.

Having stood between them long enough, Hank Ashwood was

now tired of it. He liked fun; he didn't mind fighting. But he didn't like sarcasm.

"Calder," he declared, "we don't know Pike, and Pike don't know us. I said we were mustangers, and that's the story on us. They call me Hank Ashwood. This is my partner, Red Wolfe. We'll be over to say howdy after we've eaten. Tell the lady we're sorry about the shot. We don't know this fella, Pike, and we don't aim to squat. Will you tell her that?"

"No," Ramon Calder said. "I will tell her that Pike has sent two more squatters in. But that I ran them off."

"Well, listen to the boy." Red took a twist of tobacco from his hip pocket and broke off a chew with his teeth. He began to work it up. "Calder …," he said, "Ramon Calder. Got a gringo daddy, eh? Reckon that would make you kind of a half-breed, eh?"

There was a pistol at Calder's hip that Hank had not noticed. He saw it now, gleaming in the firelight, rising from the far side of the horse as the Mexican threw down on Red.

Red's gun was holstered at his feet, lying beside his saddle. He dropped to his knees and clawed at the gun. Hank's hand and wrist rolled in a blur of fluid movement. The knife turned lazily in the air and hit Calder's wrist with such force that the pistol was jarred from his grasp. It fell into the grass.

Calder stared at his arm. The point of the knife had gone in crookedly, tearing the shirt, ripping his flesh. As the blade fell to the ground, blood flooded his sleeve.

Red had kept moving. He was across the fire, leaping at Calder, pulling him to the ground. He had pumped four blows into Calder's face before Hank dragged him off, dominating him by sheer fury.

"You hard-mouthed little pint of willow juice! Why didn't I let you have it? We could have made a friend out of this boy, maybe, but now you …" He shook his partner savagely.

Red twisted away. "He threw down on me, didn't he?"

"After you called him a 'breed." Hank turned to stare down at the Mexican. The boy was stunned, and was bleeding steadily.

With a clean bandanna, Hank bound the injured wrist. "I'm sorry about this," he said.

But the Mexican's eyes remained stony. He did not say another word. When he finally left, he did not return to the rancho headquarters but quartered off northeast, toward his own ranch.

Red found a bottle of wine that he had acquired at a mission the day before. He lay back on his blankets and tilted the bottle to his lips.

"I'll buy him a drink in town," he offered, grinning. "Hell, we'll make a Christian out of that kid yet."

"The less we have to do with that fire-eater," said Hank, "the better off everybody's going to be. If they're all as touchy as this one, we're going to have to go in with our hats in our hands before we get rid of these horses."

II

In the morning, a man from the ranch house rode to the horse camp. "Juan Soto, mayordomo of this ranch," he introduced himself. "At your orders, señors." He was slender and dark, with leathery skin and a gray mustache, an old but a vigorous man.

"Glad to know you," Hank said. "Young Calder tell you what we wanted?"

"You desire pasturage, as I understand. *La patronacita* will have to decide. Will you come to the casa?"

They rode through the vineyards. *La patronacita*—the little boss. It was intriguing, and Hank wondered how she would look. Probably seventy-five, and would have wooden pegs for teeth. Soto led them into the courtyard. Two women stood in the doorway of the kitchen, watching them.

Directly in front of them, as they rode through the gate, was the two-story wall of the main building. A gallery ran along the full length of the upper floor. Vines trailed along the spidery woodwork, and behind it, standing in the sunlight, a girl was stroking her hair with a silver brush. Seeing them, she stood poised with the brush to her hair.

He would always remember her that way, Hank knew. When he thought of the Pueblo of Los Angeles, he would think of a girl on a balcony, brushing her black hair with a silver brush. In her vivid features was the same pride Ramon had thrust at them.

Even after she had called down, "*¡Momentito!*" Hank sat, staring.

Red caught his glance. "By godlins! Now there's a Mex filly I wouldn't mind putting my brand on." Soto growled something to the boys who came to take their horses. They walked toward the big, nail-studded front door. Walking slowly, a lanky-boned man with unkempt dark hair, his sleeves too short, and his face unshaven, Hank felt like a peddler about to invade a forbidden parlor.

Soto took them to the parlor. The furniture was heavy, homemade stuff, but handsome. The floor was red tile, patterned with hides.

The girl came down the stairs into the hall and entered the room. The tapping of her heels was light and feminine and throat tightening. Both men bounced up.

"*Los americanos, señorita*," Soto announced. "They would like to arrange for pasturage."

She met them without a smile. "*Bienvenidos, caballeros.*" She was tiny, olive skinned, and slender, with eyes like black velvet. Her lips were very bright. She wore a high-necked gown of pale green merino whose lowest hoop just brushed the floor.

And watching her move toward a chair, Hank decided his first impression in the courtyard had been right. She was the loveliest woman he had ever seen.

He started to sit down again, but she raised a slim hand toward him in a motion of annoyance and alarm.

"Oh, no, you mustn't! Please!" She hurried across the floor to remove an antimacassar-like cloth of petit point from the back of Hank's chair. "It is very precious to me, you understand. My mother made it. And you Americans … the grease you put in your hair."

Deliberately she laid it on the arm of a chair and sat in the center of the sofa, adjusting her skirt about her. Then she raised that lovely young face imperiously and allowed her eyes to say that she was ready for them to talk to her.

Hank ran his hand over his hair. There was dust in it, perhaps, that a creek bath hadn't removed completely, but there was no grease. He told her as much with his glance, but said nothing. This tramps-begging-at-the-back-door role that she had assigned to them got under his hide. He decided that she would speak first.

Finally she said, "I notice that you were in the army," glancing at his faded shirt.

"For a while."

"During the war?" And when he nodded: "Then you must have killed a great number of Mexicans?"

"Only the ones that were trying to kill me …"

"And won much medals. And honor." Her voice was scornful.

He said: "Can't we agree the war is finished? I don't know who started it, but I'm ready to forget it. Our business here is with horses."

"Querida," Red chimed in boldly, "how'd you like a yella horse to set off that black hair of yours?"

"I fear the price would be too high."

Red laughed. "Wouldn't be a question of money at all, querida."

The girl flushed, from shame or anger, Hank could not tell.

"You Yankees! You think that is all there is to it … you come in here and think that you can treat us all like swine! And if we object, there are always your guns." She looked directly at Hank. "Or your knives."

"Now hold on," he said. "We got some horses to sell. We came a thousand miles to sell them, and the first night we get here a sprout tells us to break camp and move along, and pulls a gun on us."

"After he had been insulted."

"That kid gave me a pretty good roasting first, querida." Red grinned at her.

"In California," said Julia de la Torre, "gentlemen call a lady by her proper name at the first meeting. Words like sweetheart are not permitted."

Red bit off the end of a cigar. "Us gringos work kinda fast. You'd be surprised to know how we treat ladies we take a shine to, on the second meeting."

Her lips went thin as she fought to contain her anger. "You have come to ask me for pasturage. What is it worth if I say yes? Will you and Pike leave me alone? Will you—?"

"Pike, Pike. That's all I hear," Hank said. "Who is Pike? Your pal Ramon Calder pulled the same thing on us. This Pike must be quite an hombre."

She sighed. "All right. I'll pretend that you are as innocent as you want me to think. Pike is an empresario who is camped with his squatters on my land. According to law, I can make him get off. According to practice, he can stay until the courts decide he ought to have the land, if he wants it so badly. Then he pays me a little money, and I have been satisfied."

"That really how it works?"

"When one's name is de la Torre. If it were Smith, for instance, or Jones ... it would go differently. My title would have been acknowledged four years ago, and I could run off Pike before he ruins me."

Hank said easily: "Then why not throw him off ... tie a can to his tail?"

He had forgotten the mayordomo, Soto, who spoke now from the doorway.

"Vincente Arvizu was fined five hundred dollars for throwing some squatters off his place. And then they brought their relatives. He lost everything."

In the silent parlor, guilt buzzed around the Americans. Even Red shifted on his chair.

Abruptly Hank rose. Carefully he replaced the antimacassar. "I hope we didn't bring in any vermin, señorita. You go right on fighting the good fight. Enough females like you could send any army in the world home dragging its muskets."

Their eyes clashed.

"We ... we have not arranged about your horses," the girl said quickly. "I shall buy all of them. I'll send the horse foreman back with you."

He smiled. "You really don't trust us, do you? You still figure maybe we got a connection with Pike. But give us a good hatful of money for our horses and we might listen to reason and ride off. Ain't that it?"

"Do not all Americans have a price?" she asked contemptuously.

III

That morning they drove the horses five miles north into some brown hills. Here, on scorched grass ,in a dusty live oak grove, they settled the herd once more. Then they ate hardtack and venison and sat among the low-branching trees, sipping their coffee. Hank could discern the pattern of the vineyards and horse pastures, fruit orchards and truck gardens of Julia de la Torre's Rancho Temescal.

Evidently Red had been studying it, too. "That there's a tolerable big outfit. Must've been fifty flunkies around the hacienda this morning."

"No wonder pigs like this Pike try to grab off the old ranchos, eh?" Hank knocked out his pipe and covered the sparks with loose dirt. "Well, we better curry the horses. I figure tomorrow we ought to move them into the plaza and advertise 'em. They must have a paper, town of this size."

Stretching, Red smiled like a lazy tomcat. "That ain't all they got, I reckon. You take care of the advertising. I'll track us down some sweet-smellin'—hey!"

He grinned, ducking the rock Hank had chucked in his direction. They got up and went to work.

With currycombs and dandy brushes, they burnished the golden horses. Hank wished the Torre girl could see them. She would gasp, and he would say: "Take your pick. Nothing stingy about a Yankee, querida."

Of course, if she had formed her impression of them from an occupation army and one-mule sharecroppers like Pike, you couldn't blame her. Yet every time he remembered the way she had treated him about dirtying the chair, he got warm in the neck. He found himself thinking, too, about this fellow Pike, and the kind of reputation a man like that brought to other Americans.

When they had finished with the horses, it was almost dark.

"I got Pike and his bunch spotted over in that wash where all the smoke is," Hank said. "Probably cooking a beef they stole."

"You figuring on riding over that way?" Red asked.

Hank nodded. "This may be just a cockeyed idea of mine. You don't have to get mixed up in it."

"We're partners, ain't we?" Red said.

They pulled out two mounts, tightened their saddle girths, and rode out.

They encountered the fragrance of Pike's camp before they found the camp itself. Rotting carcasses of sheep, rudely butchered for a few tender cuts, lay in the brush beside the trail. Soon they came in view of a campfire and saw deer-hide tents among scattered oak trees. Riding in, they saw that a beef was being barbecued in a pit; a man was slopping sauce onto it with a mop-like affair. The scent of it was overpowering. They sat inhaling it and inspecting the sprawl of a half dozen tents among gear of all sorts—plows, saddles, bucksaws, boxes.

A man spoke from the shade of a tree. "Howdy, boys. You the mustangers?"

Hank noticed the rifle in the crook of his arm. "Yep. Smelled your food."

"Plenty for everybody," said the man. He came forward to look at them. He was tall and well made, youngish, not bad looking—a supple man wearing a saucer-brimmed straw sombrero.

"Owen Pike," he said.

"Hank Ashwood," Hank said. "This is Red Wolfe, my pardner. Might take some of that boot leather you're cookin'."

At the barbecue pit, they shook hands with the bald-headed little man with the mop. His name was Brown. There was another man named Flint who had unhappy gray eyes that watched with suspicion from beneath thick brows. Flint was very tall, with wide sagging shoulders. He had badly made false teeth that he rattled like a horse chewing a bit.

"Rest of the boys are in town," Owen Pike said, "gittin' fixed up." He chuckled.

All of these men, Hank perceived, had one thing in common. They were unconscionably lazy. They would do three days' work to get out of one.

"Aim to settle," Pike queried, "or move along?"

"¿Quién sabe?" Red shrugged. His teeth tore at a dripping slab of meat.

"Fix you up with a nice piece of land," said Pike.

"Horse traders"—Hank sighed—"can't afford land like this."

"Bring me a couple of them titles," Pike told Flint.

Flint brought some impressive-looking documents. Pike frowned over one. "This is five hundred acres. Fifty acres of muscat grapes grow on it and a hundred orange trees. The rest will cultivate or raise stock."

"Nearby?" asked Hank, with interest.

"You're settin' next door to 'em. Both on Rancho Temescal."

"You own the land?"

"Fixin' to." Pike winked. "I'll sell either or both at a dollar an acre. Or trade for horses."

"What if this de la Torre woman makes trouble?"

"You got it wrong, friend. They don't make us trouble. We make them trouble. You could move in tomorrow."

"But how do I know these titles will stand up?"

Pike drew the cork from a jug of whiskey, laid the jug across his elbow while he drank, then stoppered it again. "I get it that every Mexican title in Los Angeles county is going to be throwed out. That makes the next titles in line good. And you know what they say about possession."

Hank drank deeply of the whiskey. After belching, he said mildly to Red: "Cover Brown and Flint."

Red pulled his gun and the squatters blinked at it. Pike stared, then roused up from his heels to reach for his rifle, cocked against an ox cart. "Well, by God," he snarled. His face writhed, coming out evil as that of a cur.

But he froze when he saw the knife shining in Hank's hand. Hank reached forward to catch Pike's gun belt and cut it loose. The revolver fell to the ground.

"Get up," Hank told him.

Pike came up tall, like an Indian. He threw aside his hat and waited. His face was murderous; his eyes bored at Hank's.

"Up to you," he said. "But remember … in this town you can have a man killed for two bits, and git change."

Hank sheathed the knife and handed his Colt to Red. "You ain't worth two bits." His left hand flicked into Pike's face. His right crashed in when the squatter ducked. Pike covered his face and stumbled away. He went to one knee but lunged up again. As Hank came slashing in, he wiped the blood from his face and slanted into him, both arms swinging.

Hank ducked under the squatter's swings and butted him in the belly. He got his arms around him and ran backward. The squatter, Flint, bawled: "The pit, Owen!"

Hank unlocked his arms and stopped short. Owen Pike stared at him, afraid to look back. At once he leaned, flailing, into Hank, swearing, calling up all the vicious profanity of two languages. Hank dodged and ducked, and then feinted at Pike's crotch with his knee, and, when Pike grunted and covered up, he slammed him in the face with an overhand right. Pike's head jerked. He twisted backward and sprawled across the greasy, sweating carcass of the spitted veal. Screaming, he went ankle deep in the coals before he could haul himself out. Red was roaring with laughter. Hank just stood there with a grin, waiting to see whether the squatter had all the fight squeezed out of him.

Groaning, Pike held his feet for one moment, as he huddled on the ground. But an instant later he clawed his hands full of dirt and hurled it into Hank's face. Hank's eyes were full of the grit. He heard Red's angry bawl: "Duck, Hank, I'll give it to him!"

But the squatter was upon him, hammering one into his jaw, and, as Hank went back, he felt Pike's hand clutching at his hip. Hank felt the knife slip out of the sheath. What had been only a rough fight was now deadly serious.

Pike was moving in like a cat. Hank considered ducking away to give Red a shot at him. Yet he wanted to handle this himself, and he did not want anyone killed. He wanted Julia to know that he had been enough, bare-handed, for a whole camp full of squatters.

The knife cut the air before his belly, withdrew, slipped in toward his breast, retreated again. Hank backed slowly. Then Pike dived in with a straightforward lunge for the buckle of his belt. Hank jumped sideways and brought a smashing fist down upon Owen Pike's forearm. The knife fell. Hank scooped it up, and, as the squatter went for his throat—he brought it across the side of his head.

The tip of the squatter's ear fell to the dirt. Blood fountained over the side of his head and down his neck and shoulders. When Pike saw the bit of flesh in the dirt, he covered his ear with his hand and staggered away. He sat on a log with his palm against his ear, twisting his head back and forth in agony.

Hank saw to the disarming of the other squatters. He carried all their pistols in his hat. Mounted, he stopped beside Pike.

"You got all day tomorrow to pack and get. Be gone the next morning. Or all the two-bits in Los Angeles won't keep you from losing the rest of that ear."

IV

The pueblo called the Queen of the Angels was different from anything Hank had ever seen. It was a long haul from an Eastern town, or even Santa Fe. Nothing seemed to matter to the natives. Even the air was soft and slow.

They had moved into town the day after the fight, and pitched camp in a vacant lot off the plaza, under a huge peppertree dripping red. They corralled the horses in a rope enclosure and Hank put an ad in the *Star*, and the horses began to sell. They did not make $100 a head, but they did well.

Red and Hank took their meals in a Mexican café on the plaza. In the evenings they would sit in the deep bay of the windows, smoking and watching the traffic come and go, and, after a while, when it was dark, Red would say: "Got to find a gal, Hank. I'm great for dancing." With a laugh he would go out into the night. After a couple of these nights he asked Hank: "What's eating you, compadre? All the señoritas you were going to swing, and you ain't done anything but eat and work since we hit town."

"Anything wrong with eating and working?"

"Nothing wrong with the fillies here, either. Tell you one thing … they ain't the angels they named the town after."

And Hank sighed and wished he could get the picture of a black-haired girl out of his mind.

At 8:00 p.m. one night, as he was finishing his cigar before the café, Hank saw a turnout flash up to their camp and stop. He sauntered over, hopeful of a customer. A young fellow was walking nervously about the camp, looking at the horses, and, as Hank came up, he ducked to glance into the low deer-hide tent.

"*¡Aquí estoy!*" Hank called.

The man turned quickly. It was Ramon Calder. He came toward Hank with the stiff-legged strut of a small dog guarding a large yard. Hank smiled to himself, but his hand was on the butt of his gun.

A girl spoke, close to Calder: "Ramon, you promised!"

A tingle chased itself along Hank's spine. Her voice—it was like a bell heard softly on a warm evening. He had heard it for days, saying things that tantalized and infuriated him. Now he did not turn to look at her, sitting in the rig, but watched the *Californio* come on. Ramon stopped three feet away with his hands on his hips. *Just a kid*, Hank thought. *A spoiled and hot-blooded kid, but a scrapper*. He found himself liking him.

Before Ramon could say anything, Hank remarked: "Sorry about the arm, Ramoncito. That pardner of mine … I blame him as much as you."

"What's the plan now? To lay claim to the plaza?"

"Sell and git." Hank smiled. "Tell you what I'll do. Give you your pick of the horses for half price."

"Would that apply to me, too?" asked Julia de la Torre.

Hank took his eyes off Ramon and let himself relax. The night and her voice combined to disarm him. He heard his voice say quite distinctly: "No, ma'am. I'll just give you one. To set off that black hair of yours."

"Señor Ashwood," Julia said quietly, "I am sorry about the other day. But when you are about to lose everything … I am going to accept the horse, with thanks. Ramon, will you pick out one for me?"

"Be assured the horse won't be free," Ramon said darkly. But the girl smiled and made a face at his concern, allying herself by the small action with Hank. She got down from the turnout, holding out her arm for him to take.

They stood close together. In the dying light he could see that her lips were smooth as lacquer, that there was the slightest blemish near the corner of her mouth. And that her eyes were very dark brown, with incredibly long lashes. Her nose was delicate, perfectly fashioned. He was glad for that tiny mole; without that to break the perfection, he had a feeling that he would have choked on this lump in his throat. She was sure something for a man to run smack into after five months among the squirrels.

"I want to thank you for trying to frighten off my squatters," she said. "It was very brave of you."

He felt the movement of her hand in his and remembered only then to release her. "It was very practical business, too," he told her. "Best way to show people here that I'm not like Pike, and that I want no part of Pike or his kind. My horse sales have been going well."

"Of course, señor. Good business, as you say. Pike and his men are still here, though. You must watch out for them."

"I'll take care of myself. Is that what you wanted to talk about, señorita?"

"To thank you, yes. And …" Her luminous eyes met his briefly, and he saw a doubt, a question in their depths. "Yes, there is something else. But I do not know if I can make you see." She took a deep breath, swelling the merino gown. "This … this place is not what I remember from my childhood. What we had here before the war … it used to be so wonderful! The ranchos, the people … all of us living as we were meant to live. My grandfather would have fiestas you wouldn't believe! Those were the happy times, señor!" She seemed to dream over it. "And now we have the great ranchos being broken up, the land stolen from its owners. Did you know this town before, Señor Ashwood? The fine residential district of the north side … it is now the infamous Calle Desesperar!"

Hank had seen it—the lowest part of the worst section in town. The Alley of Despair. It was the bottom of the keg, where the lees went fetid. Drunkards and murderers roamed its sordid length.

"We did not have it before the Yankees came," she said. "I have heard they kill at least one man there every night. The big hacendados have the drunks rounded up by deputies and shang-haied to their ranches, work them until they drop, and send them back with a dollar."

"All towns get worse as they get bigger," said Hank. "The town will get sick to its stomach one of these days. It'll purge itself with a vigilante committee."

"We are losing what we had. The Rancho Temescal will be taken from me. Owen Pike and his squatters will claim still more of my land, or the survey commission will write a letter to Washington saying that my title was one of the fraudulent ones given when we were losing the war."

"It can't be that bad," he protested.

"It is," she said. "But there is a way for me still to protect what I have. If I marry an American."

For an instant he was shocked to silence. Then: "What kind of fool idea …?"

"But of course! With a bona fide American name … the wife of an American … my title would be accepted tomorrow. That is the established policy. But I could not marry a man I couldn't trust. He must live up to his part of the bargain, or I would be even worse off."

"Bargain?"

"I could not pretend there was love, where there is not," she told him. "I would want him to marry me and … and then leave. Go from California for at least a year, so that I could divorce him for desertion. By next week, when the survey commission leaves, my title would have been accepted."

His face grew bleak as he stared down at her. "You don't think much of us, do you?"

"But you see," Julia said quickly, "I would pay for his name. Two thousand dollars! For his name and his promise."

"Would a Mexican do that for an American woman?" Her eyes, shifting quickly, gave him the answer to that. "Of course not!" His voice lashed her. "He'd be too proud. But a Yankee ..."

Before she could move, he pulled her roughly to him. His lips caught hers as she tried to shape a word of protest; she struggled, and then she relaxed against him. What had been meant to be a gesture of scorn did not remain one, and Hank released her, angry at himself.

He left her standing there, one hand held out as if to draw him back. "Ramon!" he called. "You better come get the señorita. She's ready to go home."

V

He told Red about it that night. Red was feeling pretty good.

"You mean that nice piece of Mex fluff wanted you to marry her and you turned her down? I'm telling you what's the truth, Hank. You ain't got the brains God put into a billy goat. Saying no to something ripe as all that!"

Hank snorted. "It's not a real marriage. Some idea about a bargain ..."

"Bargain's the word, sure." The redheaded mustanger smacked his lips theatrically. "It'd be legal ... and soooo nice. So very, very nice. *Youeeeeah!*"

"Damn it," Hank said, "A man that would do a thing like that would be so morally irresponsible he'd be a menace to society." His partner's refusal to be serious about it annoyed him. "He wouldn't only be making a pimp out of himself. He'd be making every other American in California look like one. Every Mexican widow, or single girl like this one, would be buying a Yankee husband and hustling him out of the state. Pretty soon we'd be stepping off the sidewalk for them."

"Man, you're talking like a preacher again. Must be something this California air brings out in you." In the darkness of the tent Red's cigar glowed briefly. "All depends now, on who hustles who. There's nothing says a man's got to get out of the state once he's tied the knot legal to a Mex gal. A man could do himself right proud with one of these here ranchos. Maybe even turn it into cash … Build himself a palace in San Francisco …"

Red's voice trailed off. He began to snore. Hank got up, took Red's cigar out of his limp fingers, and tossed it outside. He left the tent flap open to air out the heavy odor of the cheap whiskey that rose from his partner's body.

Sleep, for Hank, was a long time coming. He chased it down a lonely road, where the smells that came off the trees were the tantalizing odor of Julia's raven hair, where the hoof beats beneath him were his own pounding heart.

In the morning, Red groaned and held his head as he struggled with his coffee. Some men from a livery stable came by to look at horses, and Hank was busy.

Sometime after noon, Red said morosely: "My stomach ain't speaking to my throat. Hank, I don't know what I was drinking last night, but it sure peeled the lining. Nothing will fix a belly like mine but good whiskey. Hold 'er down while I'm gone, eh?"

Very late, Hank did not know when, Red was back. He was cold sober. He went right to sleep.

But the next morning Hank knew something was wrong. Red fooled with his breakfast until the mustached proprietor, cracking his knuckles, asked: "¿Demasía pimienta, quizas?"

"Nothing wrong with the chuck, dad," Red said. "Something wrong with me."

"What's the matter?" Hank asked.

"Had a bellyful of town, that's all. I'm broke, Hank. Now I'm itching to travel."

"Where?"

The redhead hesitated. "Why ... *uh* ... up to the north. North California ... the mines!"

"And you're leaving today. Is that it?"

"That's it. Sell you my interest in these plugs for a hundred dollars."

"Deal," Hank said. "Some advice, kid. Slow down. We worked like hell for that money. Save a little of the next you get and stick it in the bank. Or you'll wind up in Calle Desesperar."

Out of the octagonal gold pieces Hank put down, Red tossed one back. "Make you a bet, *amigo*. Five years from now I'll be wearing better clothes than you are. And eating better."

Hank smiled. They drank a half bottle of wine on it, and shook hands.

* * * * *

And now it was a waiting game that began to drive Hank crazy, too. He all but gave away the last of the horses, retaining only the one he had earmarked for Julia. He stabled it and counted his money. He had $3,200, gold. He clinked it in the chamois bag. Maybe money would grease a balky land title.

The office of the survey commission was in the Union Hotel. In a large room facing on the hotel corral, four men worked with maps and scrolls and drafting instruments. They looked harried, and at once Hank had sympathy for the big, gray-haired man who was in charge. Colonel Proctor must have had every landowner in California crying on his shoulder by now, honest or dishonest. There was a fat little man doing it when Hank arrived.

The Mexican had a cowhide volume under his arm. His eyes were black and miserable and desperate. "*Seguro, Coronel,*" he whined. "The name is different, but you see, my grandfather, he was unpopular after the revolution, and he change' his name. Then my father ... he was *muy fiero!* ... he change' it back! But when he married ..."

"It'll be looked into," Proctor said. "We're here to protect land-owners, not rob them."

He began escorting the man to the door. "But I have friends who have lost everything!" the Mexican protested.

Proctor shrugged. "We make mistakes."

After the old man had gone, the colonel looked at Hank. "What do you want?"

Hank knew at once that this man could not be bought. "What's the story on throwing squatters off your land?" he asked,

"That's up to the courts."

"But it's no different with a Mexican than an American, is it?"

"Well, what do you think? The case comes up before an American judge, and the squatter turns out to be a Yankee who fought for his country and brought his family out here to settle. But there's no place to settle. It's all big ranches forty miles square. Who's going to blame him if he squats?"

"That's right," Hank said. "What if he's single, though, just a drifter?"

"Every case is different," Proctor said. He opened a sheaf of papers, frowned at it, then growled: "What ranch is it you're interested in?"

"Rancho Temescal. Julia de la Torre."

"That's different. She's all right."

Hank blinked. "But she told me …"

"That was before she was married. Her husband was in to record the land in his name."

"Oh?" Hank said. "What's her name now?"

"Wolfe," the colonel said. "Missus George 'Red' Wolfe."

Hank went out and had a drink on it. Clinking the gold piece down on the bar reminded him of what he had intended doing with his poke. Get her title papers cleared for her—hand her Rancho Temescal all wrapped up in legal ribbons and say: "Here it is, a present. From a Yankee." A real gentlemanly thing to do, worthy of a grandee of old Spain.

Hank stopped counting the drinks, and sometime later found himself in Calle Desesperar, fighting with two drunken sailors who had tried to lift his wad. He beat them both into the ground, while other drunks howled wild encouragement. Hank was filled with pain and glory. It was like the hell pictures in a Doré Bible.

Much later he was sitting on a doorsill in front of a shop. It was dark. The street was quiet. His stomach, after a sleep, was tender as a boil. What had he been drinking—lye? He was sick, and came out of it shaken but sober. .

Crawling through the low door of his tent, he halted, rigid. It stank of sweat—the sweetish, nervous odor you smelled on soldiers after a battle. Someone had been here, or was here, someone who was nervous from waiting.

Pike and his squatters, he thought.

He held himself unmoving, waiting for the first small sound that would tell him from which direction the attack would come. He had no way of knowing how many of them there were and his ears strained for some indication. In his throat was the brassy taste of fear.

Breath hissed between set teeth. It was all the warning Hank had, but it was enough. He went sprawling forward to the small noise, one arm sweeping for his gun, the other held out before him, clutching. He touched something, knocked the man sprawling, and they both went down in a tangle. There was no clear chance to use his gun; he hit the man in the crotch with his elbow and felt him convulse. They swore savagely, the words twisting into snarls of effort. Hank caught a blow against his shoulder and his hand was fast enough to grab the other's gun hand and turn it away from himself.

A sob of pain reached out to him, even as he realized the wrist he clutched was swathed in bandage.

"God dammit!" Hank said. "Calder!"

"Señor!"

He felt the fight go out of Ramon instantly and held his own gun to one side, out of the way.

"What the hell you trying to do?" Hank released his grip. "You danged fool!"

"I am sorry, señor," the young Mexican said. "I did not know it was you."

"Thought you was Pike and his bunch."

"And I thought that you were your partner, Wolfe."

Hank shook his head. "You came to the wrong corral." He turned and led the way outside.

In the thin light Ramon's face was set in harsh, hard lines. "Did you know your partner has married Julia?"

"I found out today. Only you got it wrong, amigo. He ain't my partner now."

"I did not know that. I thought I might find him here."

Hank picked a spot beside the peppertree. He sat down, got his pipe going. "You ain't looking for him to offer your congratulations, I reckon."

"No, señor. Julia should not marry an American," Calder said. "But she went through with it, and gave him the money she had promised. But he did not leave. He intends to keep the ranch for himself!"

"So?" Remembering what Red had said the other night, Hank was not too surprised. Legally Julia could do nothing to stop him. In a way, the situation was funny.

"It is not for smiles, señor," Calder said hotly, watching Hank carefully. "Julia pleaded with him to keep his bargain … and he laughed at her. She offered him more money. He scorned it. Rancho Temescal is his now, he told her, and she could stay or leave, as she chose."

"He's pretty stubborn, when he sets his mind to it."

"I have offered Julia the sanctuary of my hacienda." The young Mexican spoke with careful severity. "Señor Wolfe shall not claim her, too. Soto says that Wolfe rode out this morning to look over his property, now that he is the hacendado. I searched but was unable to find him. I thought perhaps he came here."

"Ain't seen hide nor hair of 'im," Hank growled. "Like I told you, Red and I are quits."

"Good," said Calder. "Then it will not matter to you when I kill him."

VI

Hank awakened to the sound of bells—the voice of every Mexican town he had ever been through. Near and far, they chimed and bonged and tinkled for an hour.

I wonder what I'd have done if I'd been her, he asked himself. *If I knew I was heading for the street corner with nothing left but my clothes. Would I have been damned fool enough to have trusted any man on a deal like that? Couldn't she have seen that Red Wolfe was a harebrained devil-may-care, looking for all he could get?*

It did no good to think about it. The thing for him to do was pack and get.

Accordingly he busied himself throughout the morning, striking the deer-hide tent, fashioning a bedroll that would sit easily behind his saddle. There were some things of Red's around and Hank made a separate bundle of them to take over to the Alta Vista Hotel.

"Hold these for Señor Wolfe," he told the proprietor. "If he should come in."

The man looked sourly at the blanket-wrapped bundle,

muttering behind his mustache. Hank caught the words Temescal, and something about the damned gringo who probably would not need these things now that he was a big hacendado.

He supposed Red would be just one more reason, shortly, that these Mexicans could say so bitterly: "We had no Calle Desesperar before the Americans came."

Yet weren't people like Julia de la Torre to blame, as well? With her bargain that was equally demeaning, and which offered such temptation? But the argument made him feel no better, and by the time that he had downed two glasses of tequila in a Calle Alameda saloon, the strange compulsion that burned him made up his mind.

He went to the livery stable and got the horse that he had held out for her. Rope trailing it behind his own mount, he took the road toward Rancho Temescal and Ramon Calder's hacienda.

He rode in late daylight through fields of dried mustard weed. He had expected to find the carts laboring in from the vineyards and truck gardens at Calder's hacienda; there was no activity of any sort.

In the yard the silence was even more noticeable. The smell of charcoal smoke hung faintly in the air, yet there was not the frying food smell of supper. The quiet bothered him as he sat there, trying to get some taste out of a cigarette.

What the hell? he thought, and called out, "Hello!"—waiting for a stable boy to come out to take his horse. But no one came. After another few minutes, Hank hitched the horses and went on inside through the stone arch that was the entrance.

Above the ringing of his boot heels on the tile floor he heard the murmur of voices in a high-vaulted room off to the left of the main hall. In there, he found the crowd of Mexicans, the men and women and children of the rancho, bunched like frightened cattle. Some of the women were sobbing openly, wringing their hands in their voluminous skirts; the men stood, slack faced and bleak eyed, their hats in their hands.

He caught the shoulder of the nearest man. *"Señorita de la Torre ... adónde?"*

The man pulled away from him. "Gringo pig!" he spat.

Like a spark, the action seemed to ignite the crowd. A growing surge of anger ran through the room. Hank eased his hand to his holster instinctively.

"Hold!" someone commanded, pushing through the crowd. It was Soto, Julia's mayordomo. "What do you want here?" he demanded.

"Where's Julia?"

"She does not want to see you, I am sure," the old man said. "Go from here now, señor, before there is more trouble."

"What's wrong?"

"There has been a shooting." The Mexican's eyes burned Hank's face. "Between your redheaded partner and Ramon Calder. The doctor is inside with him now. I do not think he expects Señor Calder to live."

Even as he spoke a door opened at the far end of the room and Hank saw Julia de la Torre emerge. She wore a simple gown of gray, unrelieved by any ornamentation, and her face, as much as he could see of it, was white and drawn. Tears had stained her cheeks that she dabbed with a square of lace.

He could not hear what she said to those standing nearest her, but it did not take a wise man to guess. The women's sobs went just the least bit higher, rising on their indrawn breath, in the way it does when tragedy embraces them. The men passed the dread word *"muerto"* softly.

Hank pushed his way through the press of bodies. He saw Julia look up at his approach, saw her eyes go larger with the briefest mark of hope, before the grief and disillusionment crumbled her face again. And then, as if it were the most natural thing in the world, she was in his arms, sobbing bitterly, her small body shaking beneath his hands.

"Querida," he said softly into her hair, holding back nothing of the way he felt now, refusing to admit, in this moment that brought them closer than a mere embrace, that it was too late ...

She put her lips up to his and he kissed her, a little stiffly at first, but suddenly bringing her hard against himself. His fingers moved along her back, up into her soft, dark hair; he felt an ache go all through him. He was kissing her and whispering her name.

After a while she moved away from him. But for themselves and a few ranch hands straggling through the door, they were alone in the big room.

Julia held his arms, looking up into his eyes, and he knew beyond a doubt this was the face he loved, this was the woman he wanted.

"*Pobrecito*," she whispered. "There was my pride. You do not hate the Yankees all your life and then admit, even to yourself, that you are in love with one. Perhaps if there had been more time, I could have come to you as a woman, not as a frightened ranch owner who feared the Yankee law. But I did not know what to do. The day after I saw you, I had a visitor ... Señor Wolfe. He said that you had told him you would not marry me. Your business here was finished. You and he were going away. He said he felt a great pity for me and so, before he left with you, he would do me the favor of this marriage that his partner would not."

He felt the moment of their nearness slipping from their grasp. "And you believed him?"

"He was your friend, and he seemed so angry with you, for having refused. Yes, I believed him." The tears welled in her eyes. "Tell me how great a fool I was."

"You couldn't know."

"It is all my fault. But more than stupid. I am also guilty. Of Ramon's death." She started to sob again.

"I'm sorry for that." He put out his hands to comfort her, then drew them back, opening and closing his fingers. "How did it happen?"

"This morning. I tried to stop him, but Ramon rode over to Rancho Temescal. He and Red argued. Señor Wolfe refused to go away. Ramon drew his gun. If it were not for my foolishness, this awful thing would not have happened."

"You're not all to blame," Hank said, so sharply that she was startled. "It's my fault, too." He was not attempting gallantry, but examining the facts as he saw them now. "I brought Red Wolfe here as my partner. I told him about your offer of marriage, though I didn't think at the time he was figuring to do anything about it. And I'm the one who crippled Ramon's shooting hand. Whatever blame there is, I get some of it."

He reached for the hat he'd dropped when she had come into his arms. "I brought the horse. Perhaps you can ride it back to Rancho Temescal, when us gringos are gone."

"There will be little left to go back to when Wolfe leaves," she said sadly.

"Maybe not. I'll ride over there and see if I can talk Red into leaving with me tonight."

She studied the hard lines of his jaw. "You do not have to do this thing ..."

"For you?" He shook his head. "No, querida, it is for me as well. And for the other Yankees who would be your friends. I don't think Red understands that in his own way he ain't any better than Owen Pike and his gang."

She twisted the small lace handkerchief in her hands. "But there will be more trouble, more shooting."

"Only if Red wants it that way," Hank said.

VII

Julia wanted Soto to accompany him back to the Rancho Temescal, but Hank preferred to go alone. He did not like to think of what might happen if Red were drinking and in one of his ugly moods.

He rode with the soft night air pushing back his hat brim, washing his face with the clean sharp smells of the fields. They'd had some times, him and Red, some good, some not so good. Just last spring, when the bosque was sharp with the fragrance of new leaves and blossoms, they were camped on the sand in the tunnel of cottonwoods along a river. They had hunted some horses that had strayed during a storm. There was venison and quail and wild turkey and trout for the taking.

"A man'd have to be pretty used up, not to go for this," Red had said, and he'd spoken as if he wanted nothing else out of life. Then, a week later, a sandstorm caught them on the Jornada. They worked in a blinding, choking fury, struggling to keep the herd all in one piece, while their clothes were torn to pieces on their bodies. "Anybody who tries to make a living this way should have his head patched for cracks by godlins," Red had moaned, forgetting the things he'd said a week before.

That was his way. Blowing hot one minute, cold the next. So maybe, Hank thought, he'll have changed his mind about making a big thing out of the Rancho Temescal, maybe something else will have struck his fancy by now.

The main house blazed with light but, like the Calder ranch, it was quiet. Hank reined before the courtyard gate, which was closed. He had one leg out of the saddle when he heard the whine of a slug and felt his hat spin off into the darkness.

His mount shied, but Hank wasn't thrown; it was his own idea to leap from the stirrup and roll into the protection afforded by the thick wall, away from the doorway. Gun out, he waited, but there was no second shot.

"Red!" he called, changing position, just in case.

"Is that you, Hank? Well, hell, man!" Red Wolfe sang out. Hank heard his footsteps in the courtyard, then the gate swung wide and Red stood framed in the light from inside. "Hank! Sorry, amigo. I didn't know it was you."

"Man comes to pay a sociable call and gets shot at. You that touchy?"

The redhead grinned apologetically, putting up his gun. "Thought you might be Pike, or some of his boys. Ran into them this morning, up in the north quarter, and they seemed downright unfriendly, the way they were showing their hardware. I slipped them and got back here ... Well, come on in, come on in."

They went inside.

"You all alone?" Hank asked.

Red studied him for a moment, as if trying to read the full intent behind the question.

"Yeah, Hank. Damn Mexes have been pulling out steady on me since I took over. I got some boys coming out from town. Should've been here today, matter of fact." He gave an imitation

of the old, brash grin. "By the way, you ain't offered me congratulations on my wedding."

"That's right," Hank said, "I haven't."

Red turned and led the way into the parlor where they had
first spoken to Julia de la Torre. Now, another girl—a young, pretty
Mexican—got up from the sofa and stood there.

"Go get us some food, sweetheart," Red told her. "Two platters
of enchiladas and plenty of eggs."

He flopped on the sofa, while Hank took the seat he had used
the last time. The antimacassar was gone, he noted. "You ain't been
making friends right and left, have you?"

"Ain't it a fact, though. Tell you what's the truth. I can't understand how come a nice, lovable fella like me has got so many people
looking down their noses at him." When Hank merely stared at
him, he went on. "You can't blame a man for feathering his own
nest, now, can you? Hell, if I hadn't grabbed off this place, the
vultures like Pike would've."

"You were pulling out for the mines."

Red laughed. "This here can be a gold mine, Hank." He indi-
cated a bottle of brandy on the low table between them. "Pour
yourself a nugget."

They had a drink. Hank watched the redhead take two more
in quick succession before he allowed his own glass to be refilled.
Wolfe was struggling mightily to keep the light smile on his mouth,
but Hank knew what the effort was costing him. This thing had not
gone as easily or as well as Red thought it would.

Hank shifted in his chair. His holster hung free. "Ramon Calder
died a little while ago."

Red frowned, started to say something, and thought better of it.
"Damn, I'm sorry." He rubbed his chin a while. "Hank, the straight
of it … I didn't want to shoot him. God's honor. But the little
hothead wouldn't give me a chance to talk. Went pawing for his
iron. Hellfire, what could I do?"

"You could have left before any trouble started." He got to his feet, careful not to make a sudden movement of it. "I think it'll be better all ways around if you and me just sorta mosey out of here."

Red's glance sidled up and veiled itself. He smiled. "So that's what's on your mind. The way I been figuring, Hank, was you might be looking to go partners again. Now the girl ... this Julia ... she don't mean nothing to me. You know the way I am about women ... one's about as good as the other. Just 'cause she happens to be my wife—"

"Cut it," Hank said.

"Man, you got that preacher look again. Whenever you gonna relax and start enjoying life? This here spread is big enough for the both of us. We could live like kings."

"How long do you think you're gonna last around here?" Hank demanded angrily. "How long do you think it'll be before these people get sick and tired of the gringos pushing them around, robbing them blind, deaf, and dumb? Red, get some sense."

Red laughed. "I don't want to live to be an old, old man. I just want to live like a man. Not like somebody sucking favors from a Mex gal, getting her ranch back for her from the big bad gringo and ..."

"You're crazy."

"No, Hank. You're the one's been nibbling that locoweed if you think you can talk me into giving up all this. I ain't leaving. Now, if you propose to try and make me ..."

Red started to his feet. Hank's leg lashed out against the low table, skidding it across the tiles. It crashed into Red's knees and he swore, falling backward, his hand clasping his gun. Hank followed the table in a low dive. He and Red piled into the sofa and it went over backward, spilling them upon the floor. Hank's greater weight worked for him. He landed hard on Red and held him squirming, unable to reach his gun around.

"Drop it," Hank muttered.

Red struggled to get free. Hank ground an elbow and forearm against Red's throat, cutting off the flow of curses, choking him.

Red dropped his gun and Hank picked it up.

"Let's, go."

The redhead rubbed his throat. "I keep forgetting you're a knife man," he said wryly. "You knife men are just too damn' sneaky to suit me."

"C'mon."

"You really mean it?" Red was amazed. "Hank, how the hell you fixing to keep me? Chain hobble me or something? I'm telling you, first chance I get, I'm heading right back here to my good old rancho."

"Shut up," Hank said. "You get any ideas and I'll make Julia the happiest widow in California."

They got as far as the door to the hall when the night erupted into violence. A fusillade of shots tore through the house; horse hooves pounded in the courtyard.

They heard the big, East Texas voice of Owen Pike bawling to his riders: "Burn the bastard out! Burn it all! Wolfe, just show your mangy head!"

They did not know how many squatters Owen Pike had brought with him on this raid and ride, but it sounded like a regiment. The riders whooped their horses in different directions and slung firebrands that painted weird shadows in the hall beyond where Hank and Red lay low. One torch crashed through a window in their room; it caught in the curtains. The dry cloth went up with a sudden, sizzling roar.

"He really means to burn the whole place out," Hank said.

Red grinned. "You know, I do think friend Pike is peeved 'cause I made Julia's title too legal to bust up."

"Helping me take part of his ear didn't make him love you none, either." Hank had Red's Colt out. "Partner, let's get back in business." He handed over the gun and clapped Red on the shoulder.

"Let's see if we can get the rest of that ear!"

Red raced over and pulled down the flaming curtain, stamped it dark with his boots. He snapped a couple of shots out the window at the horsemen, who were swinging back into the courtyard. "You man enough to come and get me, Pike?" he hollered.

While Red backed down the wall from the doorway, Hank dropped to one knee behind a heavy table.

Outside, Pike's voice raised in a shout: "The bastard's in there, all right!"

A volley of shots drummed through the door. Pike came into the shadowy hall but did not enter the room at once. There was some conversation, and then two other men appeared, neither of whom Hank knew. Brown, who Hank had met previously, came in. Finally, bulwarked behind the other three, Owen Pike entered.

Pike had his gun out. So did Brown. The others merely had their hands on their holstered revolvers.

"Raise 'em, boys," Hank said.

He guessed what Pike might do, and he was a move ahead of him. He had his gun barrel trained on the doorway, and, when Pike fired wildly at the table top and lunged backward for the safety of the hall, Hank's shot caught him, splitting him in the middle. Pike, still moving, crashed against the wall opposite the door and slid away.

The room was dense with smoke, but Hank saw Brown throwing down on him, and he ducked, and leaped aside. The bullet ripped a gash in the table as it tore through. There was the thunder of this shot and the tumultuous, echoing roar of Red's Colt. Hank did not need to look to know that Brown was out of it.

"Look out!" Red called. "Behind you!"

Hank spun, the gun held sideways in his hand, throwing lead as if he were scything grass. Something burned him in his shoulder, but he saw one of the squatters disappear before his fire, kneeling almost as if in prayer. The other squatter was fanning the hammer of his gun with the hard heel of his hand, and Red was answering, crouched low, weaving with each shot. They were within whispering distance of each other. Their bodies jerked as the bullets sped between them.

"Red!" Hank cried, "Red!" He used his own gun on the squatter. He drove the man down, but he knew that it was too late. Red fell heavily before he could reach him, his face drained of color. The freckles stood out sharply, like rust spots touched to wax, and the boyish mouth, relieved of all strain, was younger than Hank had ever seen it.

* * * * *

Afterward, he worked with Soto and the other Mexican hands who had ridden over from the Calder ranch, attracted by the flames. They killed the fires in the main house, but two of the outbuildings were leveled to the ground.

Hank did not remember that he had been shot until he fell down in the courtyard. He crawled over and sat against the wall, and it was there that Julia found him when she rode up in the turnout.

"*¡Pobrecito! ¡Pobrecito!*"

She lay her face against his cheek and he thought that she was crying, but he could not tell for sure. The night and all the people in it swirled in his vision. When he awakened, she had removed his shirt and had bound his shoulder with clean cloth.

He pulled her to him, and they sat together by the wall. High over the vineyards a half moon shone. There was a faint mist from the irrigated fields, a fragrance of wetness and vines that overrode the smell of charred wood.

The burial party filed past them. With his good arm Hank held Julia lightly, and silently they watched until Red's body was taken out through the entrance of Rancho Temescal.

KING OF THE DEFIANCES

I

Above the mountains the sky was as gray as a bullet. Evening had settled in with cold dampness. From where Cameron stood beside his horse, he could see long brush strokes of rain sweeping over the dark ridges of the Defiances. The trail, high in the mountains, followed the bottom of a wide and sandy canyon flanked by timbered slopes. Cameron had dismounted where the tracks he had been following left the trail, and now he knelt to study them.

He was a tall man, swarthy, with dust and whisker stubble, wide across the shoulders but fleshed down to brown skin and weariness. His eyes and Stetson were gray, and everything about him—even the man himself—had a look of solidity, of long use and serviceability.

Suddenly he heard a man laugh somewhere, and he glanced up, tense with surprise. But the sound came from some cedars high up a slope at his right. It had been three years since Troy Cameron had taken a pack horse and a rifle and gone man hunting, but uneasy memories of riding into situations too late to handle them were still fresh in his mind. Then he heard an ax strike wood with a clean, sharp bite. Again it rang in the heavy evening air. Cameron mounted and started up the hill. The hooves of his pony dislodged small slides of loose volcanic soil. After that there was no more sound from the trees, and he knew the men were waiting for him.

When he reached a narrow, timbered bench, he saw two horses grazing on the whitening needle grass. Nearby two men silently watched him jog in. One of them was leaning against a tree with an ax resting against his leg. Cameron recognized him. His name was Red Roth. For a week he had been camped with his men and his huge-wheeled log wagons in the plaza at Frontera.

The other man, the one Cameron had been trailing, was lounging on the ground, propped on one elbow, a match in his teeth. His name was Tom Doyle. He was short, broad shouldered, blond, and Irish, looking more like a saloon brawler than a cowboy. A few hours ago Doyle, who was repping for Big Jim Jackson's Anvil Ranch on the mountain roundup, had left his place in a canyon, and thirty wild cattle had broken for the canyons from which they had been laboriously driven during the roundup.

Doyle touched his hat brim in a mock salute. "Howdy, Marshal," he said cheerfully. "Pull up a rock and set down."

Cameron leaned both gloved hands on the horn of his saddle. "Can't spare the time, Tom," he said. "I'm on a roundup. Some of us thought you were, too."

"Well, I heard somebody choppin' wood," Doyle explained. "Reckoned I'd bird-dog around a spell. You boys met?" he asked. "This is an old friend, Red … Troy Cameron. Marshal Cameron, that was. Cameron, Red Roth. Timber man."

Roth nodded at Cameron. He was short and sturdy, looking like the first ax helve out of the barrel, picked for trim toughness. His hair was roan red with a dusting of gray, and cut short like the mane of a work horse. Roth raised the ax at his side and made a backhand stroke at the tree.

"This here," he said, "is some of the best tie timber in Arizona. Be a pleasure to log it out."

"When do you figure on starting?" Cameron asked him.

"That's kind of up to Big Jim Jackson. Whenever he and I get together on some things." Roth grinned like a top sergeant. There were flecks of chewing tobacco on his teeth. He had thin, slick, liver-spotted skin.

"One of the things," Cameron told him quietly, "had better be ownership of the timber, or trees won't be the only thing falling up here."

Roth frowned at Tom Doyle, then studied the tall man on the horse. "You ain't sayin' Jackson don't own it!"

"Not yet he doesn't," Cameron said tightly. "The timber you're cruising belongs to a man named Gil Becket. Maybe someone had better remind Jackson that some of us are patenting land up here. He can't come back and strip off the timber just because he used to run cattle in these mountains."

"Now, ain't that queer?" Roth remarked. "Jackson told me he held notes on all you boys' ranches."

"A note," Cameron declared, "isn't a foreclosure."

"Damn soon gonna be," Tom Doyle snapped. He broke the match he had been chewing and stood up with the compact ease of a quarter horse. Cameron, keeping his eye on him, swung from the saddle. As he came around his horse, he drew off a glove. He stopped before Doyle, and Red Roth, watching them, took his shoulder from the tree and began tucking in his shirt tail.

"How soon is this foreclosure going to happen?" Cameron asked Doyle.

"Few weeks. In a few weeks Jackson'll have his papers."

"In a few weeks some of us may be able to raise the money we owe him."

"Maybe you'd better take that up with Jackson. All I know is what he told me. He's coming back here, only he's cuttin' timber for railroad ties this time, instead of raisin' cows. Jackson's got a funny idea that having a government lease for over twenty years ought to give a man prior rights to a range. He tamed these mountains, chased the Apaches and cougars out, and then they took it all away from him and ran him down to the desert."

Cameron smiled. "Don't break down, Tom. Poor old Jim Jackson's still got over a hundred thousand acres in the desert. For a few cents an acre he had the use of the Defiances for twenty years. But now that we've been ranching them for three years, we figure he's out … for good."

Doyle winked at Roth. "Speakin' of people bein' out, did you hear how he got a hold of those notes, Red?"

"Four times," Roth said dryly. "Jackson told me three times and you told me once."

"Let's make it five," the gunman said, "so the marshal will savvy that you don't need a tin badge to be smart. There was this old mercantile fella in Frontera, see, that was carryin' too many bailin' wire outfits on the books. Finally his wholesaler tells him no more supplies until he covers his credit with mortgages. He gets 'em. One day Jim Jackson hears that the store's got that passel of notes plasterin' all this range he used to lease, and he buys the store to get the notes. So now, by Henry, he owns the Defiance Mountains from buck teeth to crupper."

His blunt features glistened with pleasure. The dislike between Jackson's new ramrod and Troy Cameron went far back, to another time and another place, when Cameron was a cow-town marshal, and Doyle was a hard-drinking cowboy careless with his gun. But now, when Cameron no longer had his skill or his badge, Tom Doyle had come to his prime.

That was what Cameron thought as he looked at him and knew that what he did now must be done forcibly but with good judgment. "That's a good story, Tom," he said. "But when you go back, tell Jackson he'd better come legally or not at all. That's the story we're telling up here."

"You ain't changed a bit, have you?" Doyle mocked. "Still tellin' folks how it's going to be. This fella used to be a real fire-eatin' marshal, Red. He ran me out of town once, when I was just a little old big-eared kid. Ain't that so?"

"That's so," Cameron agreed, looking Doyle over. "I see you've got your growth now, Tom. You aren't the boy desperado any more. We'll have to measure you by a man's yardstick, won't we?"

Doyle rubbed his jaw. A wicked delight rutted his face, a knowledge that something was coming. "How about it?" he asked, setting his feet wide. "Going to run me out of this country, too?"

"Not as a lawman. I'm a rancher now. The pay's poor, the work's hard. But I like it."

"How come you quit marshalin'?" Doyle prodded. "Slow down? Guts turn to water?"

The fingers of Cameron's right hand moved. They worked stiffly, calloused by roping. The smoothness and the swiftness were gone; they had begun to go even before he quit. "If I told you that," he said agreeably, "it might encourage you to ask something that's none of your damned business."

Doyle's grin broke. Something ugly came into the young, vicious features. Just then Red Roth walked to his buckskin horse and shoved the ax into a gun boot.

"Don't know about you boys," he said, "but I get paid for workin', not talkin'. I've got a contract to make ties for a railroad. I've got a contract with Jackson to cut trees. I reckon your quarrel's with him, Cameron. I'll be gettin' along."

"That's what I was going to suggest," Cameron said, his gray eyes cool. "That you both get along. We're not going to have our range torn up by a gang of loggers like a bear sawing a rotten log."

Doyle waited. "That all?" he asked.

"That's all."

"You go to hell," Doyle said. "We're moving Roth's crew up tomorrow."

Cameron had already made up his mind. Now he moved.

Doyle's bantering smile broke like a twig as Cameron stepped in. He tried to duck the rancher's swing and he tried to pull his gun. His hand took the bone-handled Frontier Colt from his holster, but Cameron's fist jarred against his cheek bone and his other hand locked on Doyle's wrist. The shattering blast of the gun went into the ground. Cameron felt the concussion in his belly like a kick. Twisting the gun, he wrenched it from Doyle's hand and flung it into the brush.

Balanced and slightly crouched, he waited. He knew how Big Jim Jackson would react to this. But a brag was worthless unless a man backed it up. All at once Doyle drove at him like a bull. His fist crashed into Cameron's shoulder. His rough features were white with fury. His blond brows pulled up as he swung at Cameron's jaw. Ducking, the rancher took the swing on his forearm. There was a tremendous, aching power in Doyle's fist. But Doyle was off balance now, half turned by the swing, his chin unguarded. Cameron smashed his fist up hard under Doyle's jaw. Doyle reeled back and fell into a woolly-leaved thicket.

Troy shot a glance at Red Roth. Red was standing by his horse with a tense expression, but staying out of it. He turned back to Doyle.

Doyle got up as though his whole body were sore. He looked at Cameron with his bloody face, his blond hair mussed. He staggered. Then he shook his head and started back to the fight, spitting on his hands. Suddenly he drove at Cameron, hard bodied as a wild pig. Troy sidestepped, but Doyle swerved with him, shoved his fist into his belly, and hurt him. Cameron tore away. They shuffled in a circle about each other, the dust coming up and both men panting. Then Doyle hauled his right hand back and swung a blow that would have torn a man's head off. It grazed Cameron's ear. Doyle swung a right and a left and missed. He was open again, and Troy stepped in fast to jar him with a left. Then he got a right going, pivoting on his boot to drive clean and hard to Doyle's face.

Doyle fell and hunched over on his face. He tried to get up on his hands and knees, then fell back, and lay there moving slowly on the ground. Cameron drew a breath and looked at Roth. Roth looked cool, hard, and unmoved.

"Jim Jackson's not going to like this," he drawled.

Cameron walked to his horse, feeling light-headed and giddy. Tiny points of light swam before him. "The day hasn't come," he told Roth, "when a man can move in on his neighbors without a paper of some kind. Tell Jackson that."

"Sure. Anything else?"

Overhead the first hiss of rain in the tops of the trees could be heard. Troy swung up. "Tell Doyle to collect his gear tonight or we'll dump it in the creek."

Through a chill autumn rain he rode back. The rain ended and a dripping sunset flooded the sky. He was sorry it had happened, for he was a great believer in going slow and easy. But he was fighting for his life, and to make a point. The important thing now was to work out something with Big Jim Jackson before he brought his heavy guns up and blasted them out of the mountains.

II

Night came before he reached the roundup camp on Muddy Creek. Last in the association roundup, the camp was in the bottom of a wild canyon, just at the elevation where the mountains relinquished the land to the desert. Among the trees, etched against the night by the campfire, Troy saw cowmen and cowpunchers eating their late and weary supper. Camp gear and scraps of ancient harness littered the ground. In an old stone corral bawled a herd of maverick cattle.

Troy unsaddled at the picket line and got his tin plate of food. As he moved into the firelight, a very tall old man came up. Colonel Isaac Edwards was a pioneer rancher who was always asked to serve as roundup boss.

"Find Doyle?" he asked, and then grunted, peering at Troy's bruised face. "I see you did."

"He was helping Red Roth draw a bead on Gil's timber," Troy said. "I had to let them know they weren't invited. One thing led to another."

A heavy-shouldered man in a horse-hide coat and scarred chaps looked up from where he sat against a tree. Mike Saddler's hard-cut face was pocketed by the firelight.

"One thing ain't supposed to lead to another," he prodded. "I thought you were going to bring Doyle back alive and happy."

"So did I."

"Who won?" Saddler asked. He had a jeering sense of humor that irritated Troy. Saddler, like the rest, had come to Arizona Territory when the Defiance Mountains were opened to settlement but already his ambition and steady drive had brought more land under his iron than any of the other settlers owned.

Cameron said: "It's not over yet. Just, now I'm a round ahead."

Saddler tossed his fork on his plate and looked sourly at the others. "Well, this is great, boys. Jackson will make this sound like the Mountain Meadows Massacre." He stood up, tall and black-haired, a strongly made man with tough, tanned skin and an impatient vitality.

"Shut up, Mike," Colonel Edwards said. His deep-set, tired eyes were worried. "Any damn' fool knows Jackson will make the most of this. So we've got to play our ace before he lays down his joker."

"We're holding about as many aces right now as a greenhorn in Dodge City. Which ace were you talking about?"

The roundup boss tapped his temple. "Hoss sense. We know Big Jim Jackson's in as tight a spot as we are. He owes thousands, where we owe hundreds. He wouldn't trim his herds when they took his summer range away from him. He wouldn't cut his payroll. He always had to be Big Jim, the toughest hombre, the richest cowman, and the damnedest fool in the county. Buying those notes will either be the smartest or the stupidest thing he ever did. If we let him bluff us out, it will be the smartest. But if we draw a line, I don't think he'll step across it."

Saddler crossed his arms. "You were talking about horse sense," he reminded the colonel ironically.

The colonel's eyes snapped. "Which in this case means

compromising with him. Him to have some of the timber, us to keep the rest. Us to say how it's cut."

No one spoke, and the colonel's face softened. "You know, Jim ain't really a bad feller. Just noisy and full of brag. Used to buy twenty pairs of boots at a crack. And a case of razors, so he wouldn't have to sharpen them. Big Jim. By George, he is big! Git in his way sometime and find out."

"Looks to me," Saddler said, glancing at Troy, "like Cameron's matched Gil against him. Little tough on Gil, ain't it? I'd think it would have been for Gil to throw Doyle off, not Troy."

Gil Becket was sitting wearily on his bedroll, a cigarette lax in his fingers. He was a slender young fellow, hardly stout enough for the trade. He had been just old enough to qualify for the claim taking, and Troy recalled times when he would have quit, without a neighbor to help him. Troy saw Gil gaze woodenly at Saddler, looking very young, very tired, but stubborn.

"What would you have done?" Gil demanded. "Told them to help themselves?"

Saddler shrugged. "No, but you know where Jackson will make his fight, now, if he feels like making one."

"He's going to make one," Troy said, coming to a decision. "I'm going down tomorrow and set him straight."

Saddler put his thumbs under his belt. "Why you? Because you used to be a fast man with a gun?"

"No," Troy returned, "because I'm slow with my mouth. That's a trick you learn when you've looked down enough gun barrels. Of course, it's up to the rest who goes. But somebody's got to, and I'm willing."

The men listened quietly, some drinking coffee, some smoking in the firelight. They had had a month of brush popping, missed meals, and horse falls. They had had three years of scraping to pay expenses, and they had not made it. They were not only broke, but in debt to a man who despised them.

Colonel Edwards spoke in anger. "That's easy settled, Mike. I pick Troy. Any opposed?"

No one answered, and even Saddler had the good sense to be quiet. "All right, Troy goes down to Frontera in the morning. There's enough money in this timber to save Jackson and write off our notes, too. All we need is a little stretch on both ends."

"Great," Mike Saddler said. "Let's just hope Troy don't let Miss Serena Jackson make him forget we're counting on him."

The whole camp was silent. A horse stamped, the fire popped as Troy stared at Saddler, his face heated with anger. It was tough enough to have fallen in love with the wrong girl; he did not mean to be joshed about it. He set down his plate. At that moment Gil said: "Horsebacker comin'!"

Troy turned quickly from the light and saw the shadow of a horse crossing the cobbled stream. Tom Doyle rode in, collected his bedroll and war sack, and then stopped before Troy.

"Come down to my country some time, Marshal," he invited. "Let's try that caper again."

"I'll be down tomorrow," Troy said. "Sure you wouldn't want to call it settled?"

Doyle's swollen lips tightened. "Not this season. See you around, Marshal. That's a promise." He rode out, his shadow lit by the fire.

As Troy spread his blankets, Gil came to him. The horses were quiet. The fire was a flat bed of coals, and tired men were beginning to snore. "I'm going to ask a favor, Troy," he said hesitantly. "Will you take a room for me at the hotel for a week from tomorrow?"

Troy sank wearily into his blankets and raised his boot. Gil took hold and pulled it off. "When did you get too good for a shakedown at the livery barn?" Troy smiled.

"It's my kid sister." Gil sighed. "She's coming out from East Texas. I tried to talk her out of it, but I reckon she figures she's a big enough girl to come west now."

"How big is she?"

"Eighteen. She's been living with my aunt."

"Eighteen's a nice age," Troy said solemnly. "How big a ranch did you tell her you're operating?"

Gil colored. He said, "Go to bed, will you?" and walked off. Troy laughed. If Gil had a talent, it was for making a lean-to sound like the governor's palace. He wondered how large his two-room cabin had become in his letters.

III

In the fresh desert morning, Big Jim Jackson and his daughter drove down from their foothills ranch in a buggy as black and glossy as a beetle's back. Shortly after ten they reached Frontera. The town lay on the desert in a ring of withered hills, a dry creek brushing it on the west in a double file of salt cedar. The buggy bridged the barranca with a hollow clatter and flashed up the last swing of road into town.

Frontera was a village of low, flat roofs with jutting rain spouts, of tawny earth and black shade and a turquoise Indian bowl of sky upended above it. Many of the buildings were of new and unweathered adobe brick, raw and sandy, laid since the mountains west of town had been opened to settlement. Driving in, Big Jim Jackson felt strong and confident. Lately he had not always felt that way. He leaned back as he drove, his long-skirted black coat open, a large man with leather-dark hair and thick auburn brows. His mustaches gave him the look of a cavalry officer. His eyes were hazel, quick and incisive. Massively timbered, he had a body as tough as cow horn.

He glanced down at his daughter. "Relax," he said. "You look like you were going to a burying."

"Yes, and I feel like it," Serena Jackson said nervously. She was a dark-haired, pretty girl with lively gray-green eyes and a wonderful freshness about her. As they drove into the village, she shrank into her cape. "Do we have to drive right up Front Street, Father?"

Jackson's eyes glinted. "Yes, ma'am," he said. "So they can all see us. The damned turkey buzzards sat around long enough waiting for me to go under, didn't they? Now that I'm on top again, let them have a good look!"

"Are you on top?" Serena asked him softly.

"If I'm not, I'll bet I can make it in one jump from where I stand. Papoose, I'll be ranching again in the Defiances before the winter's out. Before the winter's out," he repeated. And thinking of his coup in acquiring the mortgages on the mountain ranches, he smiled to himself. Everyone had preached law to him when the government refused to extend his grazing leases and gave his Defiance Mountains range to a swarm of grasshopper ranchers. Let them preach law to him now.

Serena gazed uncomfortably up the street which was like a pass between the cliff-like fronts of the low buildings. "Foreclosure is such an ugly thing," she said.

"So is bankruptcy," her father retorted. "I've been staring it in the face long enough to know. And whether you've noticed it or not, neither of us is geared for going broke."

"But we're not going broke," Serena argued. "Anvil has always taken care of us, hasn't it?"

"That's a fact," Jackson agreed.

The trouble was, he hadn't always taken care of Anvil. He had not cut his herds because he was sure the settlers would go under in a year or two and he would be back up there. So he had finished by overgrazing. Weeds were getting in and he was worried. But how could he rest the land without additional range? Well, he would soon have it. But there might be rough times ahead. If the scrap between Tom Doyle and Troy Cameron last night was any gauge ... But he had made his decision. Hiring a gun tramp like Doyle was part of it; he had meant Doyle to be noticed. Doyle was to Anvil Ranch as the coiled snake was to the flag of Texas. He was going back into the mountains, and they had better well know it soon than late.

The buggy rattled into the heart of the town, with Fred Stiles' big Arizona Mercantile on the right—Jim Jackson's mercantile now—and the bank and stage station on the left. Beyond, a street swerved in at an odd angle from the left. On the pie-shaped lot it created was the Pima Bar, with its broken-plastered front and low parapet roof. A wooden sign hanging from a roof spout rocked in the breeze.

Serena glanced quickly at her father as he kept the buggy moving past the big store. "Aren't we stopping? Fred Stiles is expecting you to take inventory with him."

"I've got to look in on Red Roth first," Jackson said. "He was supposed to have his wagons on the road this morning. By God, if Cameron's thrown fear into him by pistol-whipping Doyle last night ..."

"*Tosh!*" Serena retorted. "I don't think Troy pulled a gun on them at all. I think Doyle was lying to cover up being whipped."

Jackson slanted a frown at her. The time had come to make something clear. He had hoped her infatuation with Cameron would wear off, but it hadn't. "Papoose," he said suddenly, "it's time you broke it off with Cameron."

As if she had expected it, Serena looked straight ahead. They were moving along a high adobe wall on the right, the old town wall over which the town had swarmed in its growth. "Why should I?" she said. Her chin was firm but her voice was faint.

Jackson's voice sharpened. "Why should you? He pulled a gun on my foreman last night. He's squatting on land that rightly belongs to me. Does that make him a proper candidate for my daughter's hand?"

Serena's fists clenched. Jackson tried to dominate her with his eyes, but she would not meet them. "But how can you claim a man's land without going to court?"

Jackson said tightly: "A man can do what he can damned well get away with. I found that out when they ran us out of the Defiances. And I can run them back where they came from, even if I've got to rush the season on foreclosures for a few weeks."

The buggy stopped before a break in the old wall. A line of oxen shambled through. Jackson stared at Serena, his long, sunburned face harsh.

"But what if they fight back?" the girl asked.

"If they fight …," Jackson began, but he broke off. Why let her fret over things, which, if they happened, would be over so soon? If they fought, Tom Doyle would soon straighten them out as to how a Colt should be used. If Cameron thought he could intimidate anyone by pistol-whipping Doyle, Jackson would show him right here in Frontera that Big Jim Jackson could make more of a wreck of a man with his fists than Cameron could with the barrel of a pistol!

He said stolidly: "Take my word for it. They won't fight long."

Serena moistened her lips. "I … I still don't see why it should have to affect Troy and me, at least until—"

"You don't see, eh?" Jackson cut in. "Maybe you'd like wearing gingham year after year, like a hill woman. Maybe you'd like raising a crop of kids on less money than you spend on gowns. Maybe so you didn't know it, Serena," he said sardonically, "but you aren't exactly an easy keeper. You'd waste more in the kitchen in a week than Cameron could save by going without tobacco for a year. You're a rich man's girl, and God help the poor man who marries one. Or the rich man's girl who marries beneath her."

"I'll learn to be thrifty," Serena said firmly.

"Good." Jackson grinned. "And while you're learning, I'll teach my cows to eat with a knife and fork. And I'll bet my pupils graduate a year before you do."

With his finger, he flipped a little gold chatelaine watch she was wearing. "One hundred and fifty dollars," he said. "And not a nickel under two hundred for every horse you've owned, because they've all got to be blacks, with four white stockings."

Serena's lips tightened. Suddenly she unpinned the watch and angrily threw it into the road. They both stared at it, then looked at each other. She loved the watch; he had brought it from New Orleans last year. All at once her eyes filled with tears. Jackson wanted to comfort her, but he only permitted himself the softening of his voice. He had passed the time for softness.

"Arizona's hell on horses and women, Papoose," he said gravely. "You might as well know what we're up against. We're in debt to the eyeballs. If we don't get that timber, we're cleaned out. If we do get it, it'll be just like the old days again. Do you want the watch?" he asked, indicating the gleam of gold and glass in the road.

She had clenched her fingers in her lap. Looking down at them, she said: "Yes. I ... I'm sorry. I ..."

"Then climb down and get it," Big Jim Jackson said. "I don't reckon more'n a half dozen men saw you throw it." When she slowly looked up at him, he added: "Be good practice, if you figure on being a hill wife. Pride's the first piece of furniture you'll have to sell."

Serena looked away again, biting her lip. "I'll sell my jewelry first."

"Your choice, ma'am," Jackson said grimly. Big and solid on the seat, he drove into the square with its perimeter of Mexican shops and crumbling walls. He waited for her to ask him to hold the buggy team while she went back. But Serena kept silent. *So be it*, Jackson thought. *She has things to learn, and she won't learn them in a morning.*

Among some dusty mesquite trees in one corner of the plaza, he saw a line of huge-wheeled log trailers, a few wagons, and a scatter of gray tents—Red Roth's camp. He stopped and stared at her. She would not meet his eyes. He dismounted.

"I won't be long," he said dryly.

Jackson crossed the small square. He found the timber contractor beside one of the wagons in the windblown litter of the camp. Roth was drawing a cleaning rag through the barrel of a rifle. Roth tilted the rifle to squint down the barrel and said: "Make yourself comfortable."

"Thanks." Jackson smiled. He liked Roth's rough-and-ready air, the tough, whittled-down temper of him. "Tom Doyle says there was some trouble last night. I've confined him to quarters to keep him from jumping into anything today."

Roth grunted. "What's the matter with that gun dog of yours? He looked more like a puppy to me."

"That's what happens when you try to fight the other fellow's kind of war. It's a mistake I don't plan to make. Cameron probably means to stall. I mean to get going. Start your equipment up today."

Roth wiped an oily rag over the barrel of the gun. "Got papers on those trees I'll be cutting?"

Jackson's mouth toughened. "You know the situation."

"Uh-huh. Cameron's in town this morning, looking for you," Roth added.

Jackson laid his hand on Roth's shoulder. "Red, you aren't afraid of ghosts, are you? Well, don't let a two-bit grubstaker spook you, either. I've already started proceedings against those people."

Roth's filmy eyes pondered. They were a peculiar, cold blue, the whites the color of skimmed milk. "You should have started proceedings two months ago. Where does that leave me if there's trouble?"

Jackson pondered. "It's possible I ... well, I might have to let them keep the land to get the timber. I don't know. The main thing right now is cash. So I might have to compromise."

"Compromise," Roth repeated sarcastically. "That's a hell of a word for a man your size to use. Makes a man think you might be biting off more than you can chew."

"I can chew my weight in settlers any day of the week," Jackson growled.

"What about settlers that used to be marshals?"

"That's why I hired Doyle. Don't let that little pistol-whippin' last night fool you. Tom Doyle can handle himself in a scrape."

"He better be able to handle a few other people, too," Roth said, setting his rifle against a wagon wheel. "Because if I go to work for you, you ain't going to leave me on the short end of the rope."

"I'll give you full protection if there's trouble," Jackson said heatedly. "Now then, you head up there today and start cutting trees."

"OK," Roth said, suddenly acquiescent. "As soon as I get some operating cash."

Jackson frowned. "You were to pull your payments out of the tie checks from the railroad."

Roth smiled. "I know. But the way things shape up, a smart man would prob'ly keep ahead of this game. It's three thousand a month for the use of my men and equipment. I hope you ain't short of cash, Mister Big Jim Jackson."

"I'll tell you what I am short of, Red," Jackson stated. "Temper. You get going, hear? We'll talk about pay later."

Roth stood up to him as if he were not actually six inches shorter, a solid, tough-jawed little man. "I'm talking about pay now. And I say it's cash, Big Jim, or it's nothing."

Jackson's hand dropped from Roth's arm. With his left hand he pushed the logger back against the wagon while he cocked his right. He had not been called Big Jim since they stripped him down to desert range, and now to have it come back in sarcasm … Roth's fists were clenched, and he waited, set and staring. Suddenly

Jackson stepped back. He had to have Roth. There was no time to find anyone else. Roth knew it, and it made him bigger than anyone else for a while.

"Pack up," Jackson said curtly. "I'll be back in an hour with the money."

"Now you sound like you might mean business." Roth grinned.

Across the bright, cool plaza, Jackson strode to the buggy. As he unwrapped the lines from the whipstock, he saw that Serena had recovered her watch and pinned it to her gown. She smiled.

"I decided to compromise. I'll pick it up this time. You pick it up the next time I throw it."

"Compromise," Jackson said sternly, "is a bad word, Serena. Never let me hear you use it again. Compromising is the sort of luxury we can't afford any more."

IV

"I'll tell you a secret," Jim Jackson said as they drove back to the store. "Whatever happens to me, you're taken care of. The store's in your name."

"I don't understand, Father."

"Just that. If the ranch goes under, they can't touch the store. It's yours. Maybe it would be a come down to wait on customers and measure out saleratus and shingle nails. But it might beat dressmaking."

Serena said firmly: "Anvil isn't going to go under. So don't let's talk of it."

Jackson turned the horse smartly into the alley beside the Arizona Mercantile. He was uneasy about this coming session with Fred Stiles, the storekeeper he had bought out. Stiles had had the call to preach several years ago, and now, having been ordained by mail, his last link with business cut, he had sunk the money from his store in a church and was ready to preach. He had not talked to Stiles since it got out that he had bought the store merely to acquire the notes Stiles held on the Defiance Mountains ranches.

On a high platform, a mustached man in a striped jersey was supervising the setting down of crates and barrels.

"Stiles here?" Jackson called.

"No, sir. Back directly."

Jackson had been wondering how he would raise Red Roth's $3,000. If Ira Woodbury, the banker, turned him down, where would he raise the cash? He had sunk every nickel of the beef money in the store.

He dismounted. "I'm going over to the bank now. Run along, but be back at twelve."

Jackson walked to the porch of the store and stood gazing down the desert street. It was bleached with sunlight, prosperous with traffic. He dipped a gourd full of water from a barrel beside the door, and drank thoughtfully. His sunburned face went hard as he saw Red Roth jog up to the Pima Bar on a yellow horse. Abruptly Jackson slung the rest of the water in the road and crossed to the bank on the corner. He sauntered into its cool, leathery gloom. The interior was long and high-ceilinged like a boarding house hall—a wall with faded paper on his left, the wickets on his right.

Jackson moved purposefully to a railed enclosure in the rear, butted the gate with his knee, and walked in. A big man with white hair and white eyebrows was removing a sheet of onionskin paper from a letterpress.

"Hello, Jim," Ira Woodbury said. "How's the big lumberman?"

Jackson straddled a chair. "No change. How's the big banker?"

Woodbury walked to his desk and sat down. Leaning back, he returned Jackson's stare. "All right, Jim. What the hell are you trying to pull?"

"If this is advice," Jackson drawled, "save it. I go to the bank for money. When I want advice, I'll hunt a preacher."

"From what I hear," Woodbury said, "a certain preacher is prepared to give you some."

"That's fine. I hope you're as prepared to loan me three thousand dollars."

Woodbury crossed his arms. "Maybe we'd better talk about what you need it for."

"I told you I didn't need advice, Ira," Jackson warned.

"I'm going to give you some anyway. Believe me, it's well meant. Jim, I just won't believe that you'd trick an old preacher and wipe out a gang of hardworking ranchers to finance your and Serena's kind of spending. What's behind it?"

"What's behind it?" Jackson stood up. He kicked the chair aside and walked to Woodbury's desk. "Your kind of friendship is behind it. I helped set you up in this bank. I've loaned money to half the men in this town. But now that I need a hand, you never heard of me. That's what's behind it, Ira. Twenty-two caliber friendship like yours!"

His voice came back to him from the walls. He was shouting. Everyone in the bank had stopped to listen. Woodbury's face was turning red.

"I don't suppose you realize," the banker said stiffly, "that Roth's loggers will go through the Defiances like a gang plow through a cornfield."

"Maybe my memory's shortening, but I disremember any tears shed over my having to give up that range."

"Leaving you only a hundred thousand acres," the banker said. "And now you've overgrazed your range and bankrupted your brand. Is that what you're offering for collateral?"

The sight of the banker's ripe face with its fierce eyebrows and its hard jaw under flabby skin suddenly enraged Jackson. Money men. They got to thinking they were God. He planted his knuckles on Woodbury's desk and leaned toward him, his tawny eyes savage.

"Are you going to give me an argument over three thousand dollars?"

Woodbury slowly rose, his mouth trembling. "Jim, you've

depleted your land because you wouldn't bring your herds down to size. All you ever cut was wages. Yet you and Serena still live like royalty. Now you're resorting to progressive betting, like a drunken gambler. Frankly I don't think you're going to make your bluff stick. And if you don't, I'll have no choice but to foreclose."

Jackson blinked. He had known it was coming, but it hurt like a kick in the groin. He couldn't lose Anvil. No, that was superstition. He didn't want to lose Anvil. That was all.

"So you think you could run it better than I can," he said sardonically.

"No, I've got a man lined up to do it for me. But if you straighten out and follow some of the more basic rules of finance, I think we can work something out."

Jackson was breathless with fury. "Who's going to run it?" he challenged.

"I don't think it's my place—"

"Who is it?" Jackson roared.

Woodbury glanced past him at the tellers. "Mike Saddler," he replied. "He's running three times as many cows as the other settlers already. Saddler will run it with an option to buy in later."

Jackson's big hand smacked Woodbury's desk. Woodbury backed up as Jackson walked toward him.

"You short-pod penny punisher!" the cowman shouted. "So you're holding my wake before the body's even cold. Are you the one who sicced Red Roth onto me for cash?"

Woodbury came up against the rail. His face was sallow. "No, but in his place I think I'd be asking for it myself."

"You're asking for it, all right," Jackson said bitterly. "And before I'm through in Frontera, you'll get it!"

He strode outside, his rage like a wild horse. In the pallid sunlight he stood with his fists closed. His eyes trailed down the street to where Roth's buckskin pony stood at the Pima Bar hitch rack. Roth, waiting for his $3,000 before he would move …

Desperation taught a man things about himself. *I'd kill Saddler if he ever set foot on my place,* Jackson thought. *I'll cut those homesteaders down like trees if they try to stop me.*

But right now Red Roth was blocking him. *OK, mister,* he decided grimly, *you and I are going to have a little talk.*

He crossed the side street to the saloon. Dim and chilly as a mine, the saloon ran back, the bar on the right, tables on the left. A stout log in the middle of the room supported the ceiling. There was a little barbershop set up in one corner, and on the bar two kegs of whiskey rested in wooden trestles.

The saloon, run by Jackson's brother-in-law, had a good patronage of cowboys, teamsters, and a group of men in linsey-woolsey pants standing at the bar with Red Roth. Jackson heard poker dice rattle in a leather cup as Roth rolled with his teamsters. After a moment Jackson went up to him and laid a hand on his shoulder. When the logger glanced around, he said with a smile: "That all you got to do, Red?"

"It's enough"—Roth winked—"if you keep on doing it."

"Ready to travel?" Jackson asked.

"Ready when you are," Roth said pointedly.

Nate Croft, the saloonkeeper, came along with a bar towel in his hand, a short, strongly built, cigar-smoking little man given to fancy sideburns and pleated shirts. Below his rolled sleeves, his arms were short and stubby.

"Nate, two glasses and bottle of the special," Jackson said. "This is my brother-in-law, Red."

Jackson had staked Croft, his wife's brother, when he came to this country broke, had tried to make a rancher out of him. But in the end Croft had sold the land Jackson gave him and bought a saloon.

"You two practically own this town, eh?" Red Roth remarked.

Nate smiled at Jackson. "We did at one time, eh? You should have come along when Jim was riding high, Red. He'd buy sirloin steak for those huntin' dogs of his. How many pairs of boots did you used to have that you'd never worn, Jim?"

Jackson said: "I've got some business with Red, Nate."

Croft poured the whiskeys but remained nearby, dipping glasses in a bucket of soapy water. Roth picked up his drink.

"I've got a hunch I'd better drink this now," he said, "or my pride will interfere. Never like taking liquor from a man who can't afford to buy."

"I'm going to need more time, Red," Jackson said.

Roth disgustedly thudded the glass down. "Now, couldn't you've waited till I drunk it?"

"Red," Jackson said patiently, "somebody's going to mistake one of your remarks for an insult someday, and break your jaw. I want those trees to start falling tomorrow."

The big room made no more noise than a fine watch. "How can you raise in a week what you can't raise in an hour?" Roth argued. "Either your credit's good, or it ain't. Maybe you can sell some of them sirloin steaks and boots, Big Jim. How big was this burg when they started calling you that?"

Nate Croft laughed. Jackson's eyes snapped at him. Nate's brown face was slick with perspiration, and he tried to stop grinning as Jackson glowered. He came to the counter as Red Roth turned his back on the rancher. "Was that cash for the whiskey?" Nate suggested.

Jackson snapped: "Put it against what you never paid me for the land I gave you."

Nate chuckled. "Seems a title like Big Jim costs money, eh?"

Suddenly, like a coin dropping on a marble counter, ringing sweetly and persistently, a thought glittered in Jackson's mind. As if Croft had seen it, his features began to alter. He turned to walk away, but Jackson said: "Nate, I want to talk to you. Upstairs."

Jackson smiled at Croft's blank face. He sauntered down the bar to the rear door. After a moment Croft followed, up a short stairway to a hall with cracked plaster walls, a door on either side, and a door at the end. Croft unlocked the end door and walked in, Jackson close behind him. It was a small, ill-smelling bedroom with a leather-slung cot, a clothespress, a deal table, and two chairs. A green blind was drawn on a window over the street. Cigar butts lay on the floor by the cot. A small Salamander safe squatted lumpily in one corner, and both men glanced at it as Jackson kicked the door closed.

He stood before the brother of his dead wife, big and puncheon-built. A queer, wiry excitement ran through him. Suddenly his shoulder moved, and his fist crashed against the side of Nate's jaw. Nate stumbled and went down on all fours. His head clearing, he blinked up at the rancher.

"What the hell was that for?"

"That was for fun. You just had yours," Jackson said. He smacked his fist against his palm. "Get up, Natey. Let's do it again."

Croft rose slowly and began to back away, but Jackson caught him by the arm and threw another punch at his face. There was a shameful joy in the rancher as he saw Croft, blood trickling from his mouth, reel against the cot and fall back on it.

Croft sat there, his face the color of chamois. "Damn it, Jim, I'll swear out—"

"No," Jackson said, "this is just a family squabble. You and I never did get our business finished about the land I gave you. Open the safe and get me three thousand dollars, gold. I'll write you a receipt."

He stared down at the saloonkeeper, hating the cheapness of him, the tricked-up flourishes of diamond stickpin and ring and a gold cap over a sound tooth.

"I paid you," Croft panted. "I gave you all the cattle I'd raised when I sold the land."

"Scabby longhorned culls. I sold them for two hundred dollars. You got three thousand for the land. Come on, Nate."

"You know this is robbery, don't you?"

"If you say so. Just don't say it where anybody can hear you, because they'll laugh in your face. Come on!"

Croft took a deep breath, glaring furiously at Big Jim Jackson. At last he got up. He walked to the safe.

V

Cameron and Mike Saddler had left the roundup camp at sunup. At the last minute Saddler had decided to go with Troy and take care of some business. They had now been in Frontera an hour, and Troy Cameron had left Saddler at the bank, where he had his mysterious personal business. He had worn that self-important, secret smile on his face as he went in.

Not long before, as they were looking for Jim Jackson at the mercantile, Cameron had seen the rancher come from the bank with the air of an angry bull, stare a moment at the saloon, and cross over to it.

Despite himself, Cameron was growing pessimistic over his chance of achieving anything with Jim Jackson. He had left marshaling with a stiff wrist and a great patience with angry people, and because of that patience Colonel Edwards had picked him to be the peacemaker. But it took two men wanting peace for peace to be possible.

Standing there, he saw Serena come from a store, a small, sauntering, dark-haired girl twirling a serif-striped parasol. Seeing her gave him a sudden thrill of excitement and need. He watched the movements of her slender waist and slim shoulders, the swing of her gown from the hips.

Against his will, because he was a practical man, Troy had fallen in love with her. Although he was not humble about being a baling-wire cowman, he was pessimistic about rich girls who married poor husbands. He knew he could not keep Serena in coal oil for the lamps she'd leave burning; what he would save on homemade harness, she'd waste in the kitchen. But love had deaf ears for logic. He was in love with a girl who had probably never asked the price of anything in all her life. And now her father was trying to sustain his own position at the expense of Troy and his friends.

Troy sighed and started to follow Serena. But then he thought of her father in the saloon. Whatever had happened at the bank, a few whiskies would make Jackson impossible to reach. He sighed, stepped into the street, and crossed to the Pima Bar.

As he pushed through the slatted doors, he remembered Tom Doyle and stepped away from the door, from old dislike of being outlined in doorways. He stood against the rough, unplastered wall, very tall, relaxed, and looking a little tired, like a marshal making a half-bored tour of the saloons. There was nothing to distinguish him from any other cattleman except a certain carefulness in his manner. He wore a denim jacket and faded denim trousers. His gray Stetson was tilted to one side, and on his thigh hung a plain cedar-handled Colt. After a moment he moved into the saloon.

At the bar Jim Jackson was rolling poker dice with Red Roth. Roth saw him first and murmured: "Company. Mister Troy Cameron to see you."

Jackson turned without haste. His hard features were composed. "Have a drink?" he invited.

"Thanks. Maybe a beer." Troy put his elbow on the bar, and he and Jackson were face to face. "I heard you were wanting to dicker for some timber."

Jackson's wide mouth relaxed. He glanced at Roth. "Maybe. What's your proposition?"

Behind Jackson, Roth grinned at Cameron. His self-confidence was like a chip on his shoulder. A chamois coin bag rested on the bar by his glass. "The same one I made Roth last night," Troy said stiffly. "Come legally, or don't come at all."

"Coming legally won't be any trouble," Jackson said. "I thought I might do better by you than that, though. Something like you keeping the land and me taking the timber."

The concession surprised Troy. But in the end it would come to the same thing. Jackson would spoil their range and eventually they would go under anyway.

"Taking the timber," he said, "and spoiling our springs and graze. I suppose you know we're scraping the bottom of the barrel up there."

Jackson let his full dislike come into his eyes. Troy saw the purest contempt there that he had ever seen in a man's face.

"I should think you'd know by now," Jackson said dryly, "that I don't give a damn how many of you go broke. I feel about homesteaders like a dog feels about fleas."

Roth chuckled and some cowboys of Jackson's laughed. Troy's fist closed. "I didn't come to you for sympathy. I came to warn you. Don't try to move in on us without something signed by a judge."

The rancher leaned toward him, his big jaw jutting. He tapped Troy's arm. "I'll give you something signed by Jim Jackson, mister. Write this down and I'll sign it. I'm starting proceedings against every man I've got on the books! You can pay up, sign over your timber … or get out. Whichever it is, I'm coming in."

Troy shook his head. "Not yet you aren't. Foreclosures take something you haven't got … time. By the time you get through foreclosing, we'll have logged out enough tie timber ourselves to pay you off. So I figure we deserve a better shake than you've offered."

Jackson's eyes were cold as a wolf's. "Such as what?"

"Splitting the timber with you. It will clear us and give you something to buy land with. But the logging won't be done by Roth."

Jackson rattled the dice in the cup. "I hear you were a pretty important fella down in Eagle Pass or somewhere, Cameron. For some reason my daughter seems to fancy you, too. That's fine. But as far as I'm concerned, you're just a man who used to be good with a gun. Tom Doyle's good, too, so that cancels you out … if that's why your friends sent you to lay the gad to me. You can be glad I kept him at the ranch today. He was spoiling to come in town and lay you down in rock salt. Understand me, now. I've made my offer, and it stands. Take it or leave it."

"I told you," Troy said, "that we aren't taking it."

After an instant Jackson straightened. "Then we understand each other," he said. Turning, he laid a hand on Red Roth's shoulder. "Red," he said, "you ought to be seeing to your provisions. I want you to haul out at noon. Come on over to the store and pick out what you need."

Roth finished his drink in a gulp. He swept up the chamois poke and dropped it in his pocket. "Sure," he said. He signaled to his men and they started from the saloon. Jackson walked beside Roth. At the door, the others crowded out ahead of him and the rancher turned back. The light shadowed his face harshly as he stared at Troy.

"By the way," he said, "it's a mighty long ride from your outfit down to mine. So don't bother riding down on my daughter's account. She told me to tell you that."

"You're a liar," Troy said. Jackson had begun to turn away but he swung back. Troy unbuckled his gun belt and laid it on the bar, holding Jackson's eyes. He was furious but he knew what he was doing. A bluff was only as good as the man who made it. It was better to call Jackson's bluff here, man against man, than in the woods where it would be army against army.

In the saloon everything stopped. Beside the door, Red Roth watched Troy come toward Jackson, listened to the soft chinking of his spurs. The bartenders gazed at the tall man in worn ranch clothes walking toward Big Jim Jackson. Jim Jackson was older, but he was three inches taller and built like a log wedge. Jackson's eyes gleamed and he began unbuckling his bone-handled Colt. He handed it to Roth, still meeting Cameron's gaze.

"I didn't get that," he said.

"I said you were a liar," Troy repeated. "And since you ask, I'll tell you your brag is cheaper than a fifty-cent watch. Hiring gunmen and wood lice like Roth to protect you."

Jackson removed his Stetson and waited. His jaw was set. He outweighed the Defiance rancher by twenty pounds. Frowning at him, Troy thought: *You could break your fist on that jaw.* All at once something made him glance down at the gray Stetson Jackson had removed but not dropped, then he knew what he was going to do. Suddenly Jackson whipped the sombrero up into Troy's face. He charged in behind it like a bull.

Troy slapped the hat away, and Jackson was wide open before him. He moved aside, light as a cat, and, as Jackson tried to move with him, he sank his fist deeply in the rancher's belly. When Jackson gasped and hunched over, Troy brought his left in a short, hard uppercut to his face. Jim Jackson fell back, groped for support, but stumbled through the doors into the street.

He was getting up off the boardwalk as Cameron batted the doors open and stepped outside. The sunlight cut at his eyes like a knife. Across the street he saw Mike Saddler, a cigarette half rolled, staring at the Pima Bar. On the porch of the mercantile a girl rose swiftly from a chair, and he knew it was Serena. The horses at the rack began to lunge against each other. Jim Jackson stood up with blood on his mouth. He wiped it away with the back of his hand

and looked at the red smear. Then he looked at Troy and his eyes were black.

Holding his fists at his belt, Jackson walked toward him. Troy waited. He had not wanted the fight. He had come here to get away from fights and memories of fights, of men with blood on their faces and guns in their hands. But this was one of the things you had to fight over, even if the girl you wanted was watching across the street.

Jackson swung at his face. Troy blocked it, and Jackson hauled up a roundhouse left that smashed into his shoulder. It felt like a kick of a horse. Troy's neck arched. Jackson brought in his right and the pain in Troy's head was sharp and sudden as glass breaking. Then the big rancher was on top of him like a cougar dropping on a horse. He stamped on Troy's foot and held him there while he chopped at his face, and, when Troy tried to roll aside, Jackson caught him by the throat and drove him against the adobe wall so that his head jarred against it. Troy was hurt and breathless. He saw Jackson's shoulder roll and knew that with the wall at his back Jackson's fist would break his jaw. He sprawled forward, catching him around the shoulders. Jackson's knee gouged at his groin as they fell against the hitch rail. They sprawled across it while the horses shied away. Then they stumbled into the road, dusty, blood-smeared, and wary, circling like pit bulls.

Somewhere a copper bugle blared. On the edge of his mind Troy remembered that it was stage day. But his head remembered the power of Jackson's blows. You could block his swings but you could not stop them. Yet he had to stop them. He and Jackson were making policy with their fists, establishing how it was going to be in the Defiances.

Suddenly Jim Jackson, tiring of sparring, buried his chin and waded in. He found Troy's chin with a swing, and Troy sat down. Numbly he stared up at Jackson. The sleeve of the rancher's coat was torn at the shoulder. Jackson's teeth showed in a bloody grimace.

"Come on, you Texas gunslinger!" he taunted. "Show me how you tamed Eagle Pass."

"Dad!"

Troy heard Serena call it from the porch of the mercantile. Jackson gave no sign of hearing. He loomed over Troy, waiting for him. Troy shook his head. He came up on one knee and rested a moment. Then he rose and waited for the rush he knew Jackson would make. Jackson's men were shouting from the walk as Big Jim Jackson moved in to finish it. He cocked his right, and it looked to Troy as hard as a horse's hoof. He drove at Troy's head and Troy ducked under it. Jackson tried to throw his left and just then Troy saw his unguarded belly. He ripped at the slack muscles above Jackson's belt buckle. Then he smashed his left with full power up under the rancher's chin. Jackson tottered back, his features loosening. He fell, but immediately got onto his hands and knees.

Troy became aware that the stage from Picacho had stopped a few feet away. The horses snorted and stomped, lathered and nervous. Suddenly a door of the coach opened. The conductor leaned over the side to call: "Just a minute, folks! Keep your seats!"

A girl—a young woman—got out nevertheless. She was tall and blond and very trim in a close-fitting gown and a gray cape. A small black hat clung to the side of her head. With one hand on the door, she stared at the fighters, at Jackson on his hands and knees, and at Troy waiting with his fists clenched.

"Stop it!" she cried.

Jackson was getting up warily. Troy moved clockwise as the rancher squared off to him, looking for an opening but still respectful of his power. Presently he saw Jim Jackson's amber eyes glance at something behind him. A trick, he thought. He'd be damned if he'd look around. Something crashed down on his shoulder. Startled, he dodged away.

It was the girl from the stagecoach. She was holding the driver's long whip. She had struck him with the butt end of it.

"Shame on you!" she cried. "Fighting with a man half again your age!"

She looked even younger than he had thought, very girlish and very indignant. Her skin was smooth and fine. It was fresh with angry color.

He heard Jim Jackson chuckle.

"I'm obliged, ma'am," he said. "But if you'll just take your place on the walk, I'll show you how we make a man old before his time."

He spat, wiped his mouth, and moved toward Troy. The girl hurried between them. Men were chuckling on the walks.

"You'll do nothing of the sort," she said. "You'll both straighten up now and shake hands."

Troy gazed at Jackson. Jackson's bloody face grinned.

"Miss," Jackson told the girl, "I hope your stay will be pleasant. But I'm sure your Sunday school class will be glad to have you back again." He nodded at Troy. "If it will make the lady happy, Cameron, I'm in favor of finishing this another time. I don't think we'll get any more scrappin' done just now." And then, tall and broad-shouldered, still as arrogant as a lion, he walked back to the Pima Bar.

On the box of the stagecoach, the conductor called disgustedly: "Miss Becket, would you mind either stepping aside or getting in so we can finish the run?"

"Why, you've finished," the girl said. "Isn't this Frontera?"

"Yes, ma'am," the conductor said. "Do you want your suitcase? We generally discharge passengers at the depot."

"Thank you," the girl said.

While the conductor retrieved the bag from a collection behind the seat, Troy looked the girl over. *Miss Becket*, he thought. *Miss Frances Becket ... Gil's sister? A week early, if so.* He kept busy, but he could not fault her figure. It was clean-lined and perfect. Her ears were small and delicate, and he noticed how beautifully her hair grew from her forehead. Somehow he thought of yesterday's tomboy, suddenly grown up, healthily feminine and happy about it. Then he walked back to receive the suitcase.

The conductor donned spectacles to read the tag on the black cowhide valise, removed it, and glanced down at Troy. "Little heavy," he said, and winked. "Them kitchen stoves don't travel worth a damn."

Even so, Troy was not prepared for the weight of it. It fell through his arms, landing heavily on one corner and snapping a cord that had supplemented the latches. Dismayed, he saw it break open like a Bible, while articles swelled yeastily from it as though they had been packed under pressure. There was an abundance of white linen, pure as snow. But in the middle of it all lay a garment of red silk. Troy commenced grabbing things up. The girl simply stood there, her hand at her cheek in dismay. He picked up the red silk and it spilled out full length—a gown the color of flame, frosted with sequins.

The girl snatched it from his hands and dropped to her knees to try to stuff it into the suitcase. She covered it with dressing sacks, but then she could not close the bag. She was pink with embarrassment. Men were chuckling on the boardwalks. Troy saw moisture in her eyes.

"Please ... will you help me close it?"

Troy bent quickly to help her. But it was too late. Frontera would have conversational material for a year. The town had seen few gowns like this. Only recently had Frontera become large enough to support a little colony of saloon entertainers, who, hurrying to work at the Pima Bar, often wore sequined dresses like this one of Frances Becket's.

VI

As he closed the latches of the cheap suitcase, Troy remembered what Gil had told him: "She's been living with my aunt in East Texas." Maybe they dressed that way in East Texas. He doubted it. He heard Frances saying in a tone unsuccessfully light: "Of course, that ... that terrible gown isn't really mine. It was given to me by someone who thought I could use it for scraps. Of course, I couldn't, but I took it rather than hurt her feelings."

On the walk, Red Roth called: "Put it on, sister! If it don't fit, we'll believe you brought it for doll rags."

Biting her lips, the girl gazed helplessly at Troy. Troy scowled at the logger. Roth laughed, and he and his men headed across the street for the mercantile. Troy picked up the bag.

"If you're Frances Becket," he said, "I know your brother. I'm Troy Cameron. Gil asked me to take a room for you at the hotel. He wasn't expecting you for a week, or he'd have come down himself."

Quickly she took his arm. "Oh, then you're one of his 'punchers, aren't you? You see, I had a chance to leave earlier, but apparently he didn't receive my letter."

Troy took her arm and guided her to the walk. *One of his 'punchers!* That sounded like Gil. He had been playing it bigger than Troy realized. Under the wooden awnings, they moved along toward the hotel. Suddenly Troy remembered Serena. As they passed the store, he glanced up. She was still there, small, slender, dark haired, intently watching them as they passed. Troy had to release Frances' arm to tip his hat.

"Will you be in town a while?" he asked.

Serena smiled politely at Frances. "I really don't know," she told Troy. "If there's no one else you have to fight with, you might look for me when you have time."

He felt blood drying on his face. He was ashamed at having handled things so badly. He tried to tell her that with his eyes. Her chin was high, but her dark olive-green eyes were sad. She had a way of gazing at you that made you think she had never felt the same about a man before. She stirred something deep and grand in him—and here he had been fighting with her father.

"I'll find you later," he said.

"Really," Frances Becket told him in a low voice, "if that's your young lady, I can—"

"Wouldn't hear of it," Troy said, and they went on.

In the lobby of the Frontier House a mesquite-root fire was snapping in the corner hearth, and Troy placed the girl on a chair here while he went to see about her room. Trimmed logs supported the ceiling. Antelope and deer heads were mounted on the walls and Mexican rugs brightened the floor. Ed Owen, a large, ripe-faced man who arranged his red hair guilefully to conceal a nearly bald skull, said he had one room that had not been taken by the seasonal influx of cattle buyers and drummers.

"I'd better look at it," Troy said.

He used the opportunity to wash up in the small bedroom at

the back of the building. A fight last night, a fight today. He was beginning to look like a prize-ring veteran. His head throbbed. He washed, dried with a bandanna in order to leave the towel untouched, and returned to the lobby. The girl smiled as he sat beside her on the hard wooden bench. She looked clean and fine, but how could you believe such a preposterous story as she had told about the dress?

"You didn't believe me, did you?" Frances asked him.

"When I look at you, I almost believe it," he said gravely.

"Spoken like a very gallant employee," she said. "I'll commend you to my brother. In the meantime, I must say that I don't think your conduct in the street reflects much credit either on you or on Gil as your employer."

"I expect not," Troy admitted.

"I hope," the girl concluded, "that Gil won't find it necessary to let you go because of it."

"No, ma'am," Troy said humbly. *Well, let her find it out*, he decided grimly, *if I've been reflecting discredit on people.*

"Getting back to that awful dress," she said with a nervous little laugh, "I'm going to tell you the real story and you'll understand why I couldn't blurt it out. Though, of course, now I wish I had ..."

She told him another story about doing some dressmaking in Fort Worth, and some of her customers being—well, anyway, Frances made those sequined dresses for them. And one girl hadn't paid for the last dress and she wasn't going to give her this one free, so ...

"Now," she asked, "do you believe that?"

"Why not? Only I don't understand why you told the other story."

She bit her lip. Her eyes were blue and wide set. She looked pretty and intelligent, he thought. About all she needed was experience, and she was right on the point of getting some of that. "Well, I just didn't think Gil would appreciate everyone's knowing I've been making entertainers' gowns while he's been doing so well out here. They'd wonder why he hadn't sent for me, or at least been supporting me. But of course the fact is that he has to put everything back into the business. Naturally he didn't want everyone to know all his business affairs. Is he well?" she asked.

"Strong as a horse."

"I'm so glad." She sighed. "Gil was never very strong. But he had this dream of being a rancher. He wasn't going to be a teacher, like all the other Beckets. Who was that man you were fighting with?" she asked with sudden curiosity.

"His name is Jackson."

Her clear eyes studied him. "The man who used to run cattle in the mountains?"

"That's the man."

"Is there still some bad feeling?"

Troy inspected his skinned knuckles. "Lately. Maybe we'd better talk about what you plan to do, now that you're here."

"Naturally I want to get right up to the ranch," she said enthusiastically. "When will you be going back?"

"Tomorrow morning. It's a long ride and you'll want a rest after the trip. You can look around today, get a good sleep tonight, and we'll leave tomorrow after seven. All right?"

Smiling, she stood up and offered her hand. It was encased in a crisp little lace mitten. "You've been very helpful, Troy. Will you do me one more favor?" Her face began to color. Her skin was so fine that blushing must be a problem.

"About the dress?" Troy smiled. "Sure, I'll pass it around. I don't think they'd have been fooled long, anyway."

"Hurry back to your young lady, now," she told him. "If I'm not out of order, who is she?"

"Her name's Serena Jackson."

She smiled. "No kin to the Jackson you had the trouble with, I hope?"

"Daughter," Troy said grimly.

Serena was not at the store when he went back, but he found her on the corner. Coming up behind her, he looked at her slim shoulders and supple waist and the smooth flare of her hips. Her hair, brushed into a glistening chignon, was so black that Jim Jackson called her "Papoose".

He took Serena's arm, and she glanced at him and haughtily looked away. They walked down a side street under an arcade of chinaberries. Blackbirds with chartreuse eyes strutted in the road.

"I'm taking my life in my hands to walk with you," Troy said. "I was told to stay away."

"Father and his orders," said Serena impatiently. Then she asked suddenly: "Who is she?"

"Gil Becket's sister. He wasn't expecting her for a week."

"Well, she's certainly here now."

Troy laughed. "You can't beat red silk for an entrance."

Serena's eyes flashed. "I suppose, if I want you to notice me now, I'll have to wear red silk, too." She pulled her arm away as he tried, laughing, to draw her to him. "I just can't understand how an intelligent man can be taken in by such an act."

Troy chuckled. "I wasn't taken in," he protested. "She happened to be Gil's sister. What could I do?"

Serena looked straight ahead as she walked, chin up, along a shadowed wall of crumbling adobe. "Of course, you believed that fantastic story about the dress …?"

"No. She was rattled. She told me the real story when I took her to the hotel." He repeated what Frances had said. "So, you see, she's really a very nice girl."

"I dare say. At least you seemed quite contented with things until you saw me."

Troy halted, pushed her against the wall, and kissed her. She tried to twist away, but after a moment she relaxed and her arms slipped around his neck. "Now," Troy murmured, "you might say I'm contented."

Serena touched the bruises on his face. "Troy, did this have to happen?" she asked.

He frowned. "Maybe I've lost my touch. Taming men on the prod used to be easy for me. But this is different. Even if we're broke, we've got rights. We offered your father half our timber, but he wouldn't settle for that. Serena, what's he trying to do?"

"Survive," she said simply. "He survived Apaches and hard times, but his friends and his government have nearly ruined him. I might ask what you're trying to do," she added. "Whipping his foreman last night and trying to whip him today."

"I was putting up a sign. No trespassing. It's got to be understood that we can't be bluffed, even if we can be foreclosed."

Serena started down the walk again, the withered yellow chinaberries dotting the packed earth walk before them. "The point is, he's got to buy land before winter. But there's no cheap range left. Whatever he buys, he'll be held up. So he's got to have money. And I suppose we owe quite a bit, too."

Troy suppressed a smile. "Shouldn't wonder," he said.

She glanced at him archly, accepting the challenge. "You might be surprised to know that in many ways I'm quite frugal. I make all ... well, some of my own things. But, even so, there are men in this country who think any biscuit I'd make would serve for a buggy anchor."

"Try me sometime," Troy challenged. "Button me a button. Darn me a sock."

"I will," she said. "I'll make you an entire shirt and cook you a meal."

Her lips pouted but her eyes laughed. And everything he had thought out alone on Defiance Mountain itself slipped from him. It would be fine to believe he was wrong about how it was to marry a girl like Serena, becoming a second-rate partner to her father, with no opinion sharper than a suggestion, and a bad habit of tipping his hat. He saw how delicate her features were, yet how strong, how fine and expensive a wife she would be. He tried, with vague optimism, to believe it would work out.

"There's Dad!" Serena exclaimed. "He's looking for me. Troy, I'll talk to him about sharing the timber tonight. Promise me you won't get into any more fights. I just know it can be worked out."

She kissed him on the cheek and hurried back to the street. He could see the flash of her polished little boots under her skirts. He tried to picture her in a dress bought from a catalogue. Maybe she was one of those girls who could wear anything and make it look wonderful.

He wondered just how much Big Jim Jackson actually had to have to pay what he owed and expand his range. How many of the bills pigeonholed in his desk represented pure extravagance? He remembered that the Battle of Gettysburg had been fought over shoes, and he wondered whether Jackson's War would be fought over his daughter's buying habits.

VII

It was a tangy afternoon of chilly wind, deep shadows, and leaves tumbling along through the brush. Mike Saddler had left town after learning that Troy Cameron was staying over to take the Becket girl to Gil's place in the morning. Now the big man, with his hard features and his coarse black hair, was waiting beside the turnoff of the wagon road to Jackson's Anvil headquarters, west of town. Long shadows sprawled down from the high ridges of the Defiances to the foothills where Saddler waited. He had slipped his horse's bit to let it graze. He sat on one of the square blocks of adobe brick that marked the turnoff. There was a rusting anvil atop each gatepost—a typical Jim Jackson flourish, in a country where hardware was at a premium.

Now he heard the Jackson buggy rattling up the road through the dry jungle of mesquite and glistening creosote thickets. Although he smoked lazily, an impatient vitality began to work in him. He rehearsed in his mind how he would carry it off with Jackson.

Mike Saddler was thirty-one. He came from poor, east-Texas stock. For ten years he had denied himself every small pleasure to buy the things he had to have to climb. He had saved clippings from livestock journals, collected scraps of paper with notations such as "Boiled alfalfa meal good for scours"; "Hogs will root out rattle weed"; "Put sand in railroad cars instead of alkali dirt"; "Never put haystacks so close a fire will spread." And all his string saving had pushed him only a few hundred acres ahead of men like his neighbors Troy Cameron and Gil Becket.

For you made your success through people. You found their weaknesses, their vanities and strengths, and used them. Ira Woodbury was a vain man. Saddler had played on his vanity and come out with an agreement to handle Anvil for the bank. Jackson was a vain and foolish man and a desperate one. Saddler knew how he was going to use him now.

The horse came up the road with a tired cadence of iron shoes, and Saddler, tucking in his shirt tail, slipped his thumbs under his belt and waited respectfully as Big Jim Jackson and his daughter drove up. He raised one hand and stepped forward, smiling, as Jackson stopped the buggy between the square, mud-brick posts. Serena Jackson gazed at him with a stiff, unsmiling expression.

"Miss Serena," he said, "you don't have to look at me like I was a highwayman. If there's any highway robbery going on, it's no doings of mine."

He chuckled and gave Jackson a friendly salute. The big man looped the lines around the whipstock and leaned forward with his elbows on his knees.

"Well, that's reassuring," Jackson said dryly.

"I wanted to talk to you about some of the things that are going on," Saddler said seriously. "Some of the men were a shade proddy when we left camp this morning. After Cameron turns in his report, now, it's hard to say what will happen."

Serena made a small sound and turned to her father. "Dad, will you drive on?"

Puzzled, Saddler frowned at her. His eyes followed the gentle curve of her bosom. Her features were neat and perfect, with a tiny scar above one eyebrow. She was beautiful, and he thought of crushing her shoulders in his hands.

"I reckon we owe Mister Saddler the courtesy of listening to him, missy," Jackson said severely. From under thick auburn brows he glanced at the other man. "As a guess, what would you say is going to happen?"

Saddler put one boot against the hub of the wheel. In his mind he selected his words meticulously. It was hard to say, *Hurt them, don't hurt me*, without sounding too blunt. "Maybe nothing will happen," he suggested, "if I go to work on it."

"How's that?"

"I mean, if I sell them on the idea of going slow." Saddler grinned. "Most of the boys are good pack horse stock. They lead fine. If I back out on fighting you … say I want to get legal advice first, something like that … they'll all back down. By the time they decide to go to war, the war will be over. You'll have your papers in shape. The law will be on your side."

"That figures," Jackson said thoughtfully. "But what about Cameron? I thought he was the boss man."

Saddler shrugged. "Colonel Edwards sends him to town to make peace, and he comes back lookin' like hell wouldn't have him. I don't reckon Cameron will be much of a problem," he finished.

He watched Jackson lift the buggy whip and frowningly pop it at a tuft of grass. He was big. My God, he was big! Wonder he hadn't killed Cameron. His fists were like walnut burls, and that chin of his was an anvil. But he wasn't big in cow savvy, and he was a fool about money. As Saddler thought of his deal with Woodbury to manage Anvil after Jackson went under, something like woman hunger tingled in him, obsessive and exciting. To manage all that land—to have first crack at it someday!

"You know what I don't figure?" Jackson said abruptly. "What you get out of this."

Saddler stared boldly into his face. "You can clear my land …

cancel my note." He shot a look at Serena, whose expression of suspicion was giving away to disdain. "Maybe it sounds rough," he conceded. "But half the men up there are going to fail anyway. That's the history of this kind of land. What's the difference who picks up the pieces when they drop?"

Suddenly Serena rose. "I think this is the most hideous thing I ever heard! Father, aren't you ever going to stop him?"

Saddler's body cramped with shock. Jackson jumped down and walked toward him, the whip doubled back over his shoulder. Then at last he knew that the rancher had been playing with him. Woodbury had spilled it! Saddler's hand dropped to his revolver. His anger took shape, like steel.

Jackson grinned like a wolf. "I just wanted to know who thought of putting you on Anvil. You or all of them. So's I'd know how many to horsewhip. Aren't you even going to leave me five acres along the river to raise chilies?"

"Five acres?" Saddler mocked, his dark, muscular face scornful. "You'll finish with nothing. Big Jim! There's nothing big about you but the mistakes you've made. Read the writing," he scoffed. "Without our trees, you can't pay the bank. And you won't cut a tree while any of us can pull a trigger."

"Won't I?" Jackson retorted. "Be at Pine Meadow after Roth moves up and you'll see me skin your ranch out like a jack rabbit. So you were going to slow me down, were you, until the bank was ready to take over Anvil? I'll show you how I slow down the likes of you!"

In a quick rush he moved in to slash at Saddler's wrist. Saddler yanked his Colt, but the stiff plaits of leather snatched his arm and Jackson yanked him off balance. The Colt roared—a blast of sound that deafened and stunned. The horse reared, and Serena had to snatch at the lines. Saddler yanked back, but Jackson twisted the gun away. Saddler hauled his arm free and threw an overhand punch into the rancher's face. It struck heavily, and Jackson stumbled. Recovering, he sent the whip hissing forward again. The plaits whipped Saddler's Stetson off and flayed his neck. He stepped back but collided with an adobe gatepost.

Jackson began to slash at him, the leather tearing Saddler's jacket, burning like an iron across his ear. Saddler ducked his head and waded in, caught the whip and crashed against Jim Jackson. He locked his arms to his sides and drove him back against the buggy. They fell to the ground and Saddler searched frantically for his gun. They rolled under the buggy, and, as the horse began to rear, they separated and crawled from under the wheels. Saddler scrambled up with Jackson still on his knees. He was afraid now, having felt Jackson's strength and knowing he could not match it. He gazed about for a weapon of some kind. Then he saw Big Jim Jackson rising from the ground with a stone as big as an anvil in his hands. Jackson came toward him, raising the stone to chest height.

Saddler's mouth twisted. "Don't," he gasped. He began backing but came up against the gatepost. Jackson kept coming. In the buggy, Serena turned her face away. Abruptly the rancher tossed the rock at Saddler. He arched it across the few feet separating them, but for some reason he did not hurl it with force. He was merely tossing it to the settler. The stone dropped toward Saddler's belly, and he hunched as he braced himself to catch it. When he caught it, it bore him to his knees.

Jackson lunged in swiftly, smashing at the rancher's head as he dropped the stone, his right fist thundering against Saddler's ear, his left crashing against his jaw. Finally there was a hard, clean blow to his chin. Everything in Mike Saddler's vision had a glistening soap bubble shimmer for an instant. Then the brightness burst, and Saddler felt himself drowning in blackness.

* * * * *

When Saddler came to his senses, the Jacksons had gone and it was almost dark. He lay face down between the gateposts. Saddler painfully sat up and a strong breeze blew on his face and began to restore him. At first it was all pain and dullness. But then his mind started putting it together, and he struggled to his feet and rolled a cigarette and knew before he had lighted it the impossible situation he was in.

If Cameron still worked out the compromise he had been talking about when Saddler left town, Mike Saddler was on his own. Jackson was going to clean him out. Irrespective of any deal with the others, he would clean him out to square for Saddler's arrangement with the bank.

Standing there in the mesquite, the night wind off the desert stirring his long coarse hair, he felt desperately alone. How could one man buck Jim Jackson, Red Roth, and that poisonous little gunslinger, Tom Doyle? Saddler drew on the cigarette grimly, going through his cards like a poker player. He had thought himself finished with the Defiance Mountains crowd—those small, bungling ranchers. But now he realized he had to have them. They were the only allies left to him.

With cold alarm, he knew that, if the others compromised with Jackson, he himself would be left out. That could not happen. Cameron with his compromise talk had to be stopped cold.

In the clotting shadows of the brush, Saddler found his bridle, bitted up his pony, and started up the wagon road into the Defiances. He was weary and shaken, but his desperation was beginning to scale away. With bitter logic he considered what had to be done. Cameron and the rest must be put into a frame of mind where they would stop talking compromise. At the same time, Jackson's will to break them had to be made even stronger.

When he had ridden a couple of miles, he decided how it could be done. But he could not manage it alone. He would need help. All right, he had two cowpunchers. Let them start earning their pay.

As it grew dark, Saddler let the horse push along without reining. The road crested before dropping into Pine Meadow. Saddler looked down on the long, winding valley toward his ranch, tasting the cold wind. Below him and at the north end of the valley he saw the light—a lonely spark lying in blackness. Saddler's two cowpunchers were at the cabin, keeping things going while Saddler followed the mountain roundup.

The cabin lay at the edge of the timber. In pole corrals some horses whickered and Saddler's horse trembled and trumpeted back. Saddler smelled the rotting carcass of a calf. *That damned Wiley*, he thought. Wiley was his half-Basque cowpuncher. Basques never felt comfortable without some meat rotting near them. Inside the cabin the lamp went out suddenly and something was laid on a windowsill.

"That's far enough!" a voice called.

"It's me," Saddler retorted. "If it was anybody else, you'd have your heads shot off by now. Git out here and fork up some hay for this horse."

The rusty shade of a storm lantern grated up and the Basque came out and turned the beam on Saddler. "What the hell happen?" he asked, staring at the rancher's cut face.

Saddler grimaced. "Jackson and Doyle bushwhacked me. Where's Bill?"

"Inside. What the hell they bushwhack you for?"

"Feed the horse and get inside," Saddler ordered.

Bill Thorne was pulling on old stovepipe boots as Saddler tramped inside the cabin. He gave Saddler a nervous grin of greeting. Thorne was a wiry man of about thirty with a wizened, ugly face; he looked very cagey, but he wasn't. He had ambition but no ability; he thought he had much in common with Mike Saddler because he had foolish dreams of being a rancher. Thorne missed the difference between dreams and plans.

Saddler threw his hat on a cot. Standing hands on hips, he glared about the main room of the three-room cabin.

"This layout," he said disgustedly, "looks like a sheepherder's convention had just broken up."

Thorne grinned. "Yeah, well, we were going to swamp out tomorrow, Mike."

Saddler gave him a crooked smile. "Bill, you ought to make out a list of things you're going to do tomorrow. Gonna make you a pretty full day, you know."

"Getcha some coffee," said Thorne, hastening, in long underwear and boots, to the sheet-iron stove where a blue enamel coffee pot thumped.

Saddler lay back on the cot, frowning. Thorne brought the coffee. "Did you say you had a run-in with somebody?" he asked, regarding Saddler's cuts.

Saddler repeated what he had said to Joe Wiley. "It's comin', Bill. There's no gettin' away from it. Jackson's turning his guns on us."

Wiley came in, set the lantern beside the door, and stood looking at Saddler, a tall man with a warped shoulder, slender and dark as a cheroot. His was the mind Saddler had not entirely plumbed, but he thought he knew enough about the Basque to risk saying what he had to. Wiley was a capable cowboy, long-lasting in the saddle, willing to take a chance. He had a short neck, flattened features, and skin the color of a penny.

"What's comin'?" he asked.

"The big scrap," Saddler said. "Jackson and Doyle could have killed me, instead of drug me off my horse and whipped me. This was just a warning. I was supposed to run right to Cameron and the others and tell them it was time to clear out."

"Going to do it?" Thorne asked.

"What's the use? I can fumble around alone as well as with them. There ain't a man among them knows how to fight."

The Basque cocked one eyebrow. "Cameron," he said.

"All right, but he can't carry them all on his back. No." Saddler ruminated, shifting on the cot. "I'm going to give them something to fight about. Both sides ... Jim Jackson as well as those hayseed compadres of mine."

Thorne brought a tin cup of coffee and set it on the floor. He put one foot up on a stool and peered at the rancher. There was silence. Saddler met his eyes boldly, then looked at Wiley again and waited for one of them to ask it. But no one spoke.

"Can you keep your mouths shut?" Saddler asked.

Bill Thorne hunched forward on the stool. He liked secrets. Tell him you had a secret reason for it and he would pack a cow ten miles on his back.

"I've got a deal on with Ira Woodbury," Saddler said. "Woodbury figures Jackson will go under. He's picked me to ramrod Anvil for the bank after he forecloses."

"Fact?" Thorne whispered, his dark monkey's face eager.

"Looks like my cue to make sure Jackson goes under, don't it?" Saddler chuckled.

"Yeah," Thorne whispered.

Saddler glanced from him to Joe Wiley. The Basque was listening, half smiling. Saddler sipped some of the acrid coffee. "You men want to be knot-head cow prods all your life?" he asked. "Or do you want a shot at owning your own irons some day?"

"All my life …," Thorne began huskily.

But Saddler interrupted: "Joe, you ain't talking much."

"Listenin', though." Wiley smiled.

"Likin' what you hear?" Saddler asked.

"Int'restin'."

"OK. If you come with me, I'll let both you boys keep your own brands when I take over Anvil. You can take out part of your pay in calves and just pay the bank for the graze you use. I've got an option to buy the ranch someday, if it all works out. Savvy? Stick with me and one of these days we'll all be carrying bankbooks."

"That sounds like blood money," Wiley commented.

Saddler shook his head. "Well, we may have to half kill a couple of people, like Jackson did me. I want Jackson to be mad enough to eat those settlers whole. And I want the settlers sore enough to take pot shots at Jackson and Red Roth. Me? I'll sort of string along with the settlers, until it begins to get smoky."

"Us?" Wiley asked.

"Well, suppose I want you to help me burn some cabins." Saddler grinned. "Ain't afraid of fire, are you?"

"Love it," Thorne said. "Saints, Mike, you mean that after they dust each other off an' the bank forecloses Jackson …?"

"I mean you've got a job at twice the pay you're drawing now," Saddler snapped. "You get to keep a brand. Thing is, I ain't asking you to do anything I won't be right there doing myself."

Wiley's dark face still kept its own counsel. Suddenly Saddler was irritated.

"Get out, then, if you don't like the deal," he told the Basque harshly. "Joe and me can handle it."

"I was just thinkin', Mike," Wiley said. "This cabin burning sounds risky."

"At night? With the owners gone and too poor to leave anybody on the place?" Saddler rose, ambition and a vicious desire for retaliation tormenting him. "Easy as strikin' a match. But the devil of it is there's so little time. Red Roth's moving in tomorrow. We can't let those logs start going out. Once Jackson's makin' money, hell won't have us."

Wiley's slow, sour smile broke his lips. "Then we better not let him make no money, Mike. We better dig a little pit for the hound and the badger to fight in, eh?"

Saddler slacked onto the cot, relieved. Wiley was intelligent and tough; best of all, he was not weighted down with scruples. Saddler raised a boot and thrust it at Thorne. Thorne took hold of it and helped tug it off.

"Tomorrow?" he asked.

"Tomorrow night," the rancher said. "Tomorrow I'm going to be busy. Cameron's packin' Becket's sister in to Becket's place. Somebody ought to be around to welcome them. Nothing like a scared female to start settlers moving out."

VIII

"You shouldn't have horsewhipped him," Serena told her father again.

A fire burned on the hearth in the low-ceilinged room. They sat at the heavy, fumed-oak dining table. Beyond small windows set in adobe walls three feet deep the night was cold and moonless. Jim Jackson ate steadily, knife in one hand, fork in the other.

"No," he agreed, "I should have shot him."

Serena sat with both hands about her coffee cup, a light shawl thrown over her shoulders. She had been cold all evening. Her father was packed and ready to travel. He was going to Pine Meadow to be there when Red Roth's wagons started coming in tomorrow. The loggers had left Frontera that afternoon.

"When will Roth start cutting trees?" she asked her father.

"Directly."

"Is there any reason," she asked, "why it must be so soon?"

Jackson wiped his mouth and dropped the napkin. He gave her a dry glance. "Yes. Because I can't sell them until I log them out."

He went to his room and returned with his Stetson on the back of his head and a heavy-caliber rifle in his hand. He laid an envelope before her.

"What is this?" Serena asked.

Jackson opened a compartment in the big cabinet against one wall and found inkwell and pen. "Power of attorney," he said gruffly. "I might as well have it when I go up. Just to be sure."

"Oh … on the store," Serena said. And a tiny bell tinkled in her mind. "In other words, since the mortgages are in my name, you need permission to act on my behalf."

"You're quick, Papoose," Jackson commented.

He locked the loading lever of the rifle down, ran his little finger into the chamber, closed it, and filled the loading tube.

"You know," the girl said briskly, "I believe I'll go up tomorrow myself."

"Don't be ridiculous," Jackson snapped.

"I've camped before. I'm a good camper."

"You know what I mean. There may be—"

Brushed by the lamplight, Serena's face showed color. Her eyes, under the slightly quirked brows, were lively. "Dad, there doesn't have to be trouble if everyone gives a little. No one wants to fight."

Jackson supported the rifle on his palm. "Papoose, did I waste my money educating you? I know to the nickel what that timber will bring. We'll have no triflin's money left after we buy the range and stock it."

"I don't believe it," Serena pouted. "I think we could get by on much less."

Jackson's face hardened as he looked at his daughter. "Did Cameron tell you to say that when you were sneaking down that back street with him today?"

"You don't have to talk like that to me," Serena said. "I must say he talked more reasonably than you do."

Jackson's hands clenched the rifle as he glared at her. "He'll talk us right into the poorhouse, I'm thinking. Maybe I'd better talk to you a little bit myself. You know, when you picked that watch up out of the dirt today, I learned something about you. When the time comes to choose between pride and money, maybe it'll surprise you which you'll take. It won't me."

She put her hand over the little watch on her breast. "It would have been wicked to leave it."

Jackson smiled disdainfully. "It was wicked to throw it. But most girls would have let it lay, rather than march back in front of all those loafers and pick it up out of the street."

She met his dark ironic gaze, but could not answer him. She did not know why she had gone back for the watch. She had other watches, but this one was so lovely and new.

"I'm going to have Vicente load my horse," her father said. "Have that paper signed when I come back."

Her voice caught him at the door. "You're wasting your time going up, Dad. I'm not going to sign it."

Jackson came back in four strides. He caught her wrist. His face was swarthy with anger.

"Serena, this has been a bad day. Don't fret me with foolish jokes."

"I'm not joking. Before you do anything, I want to talk to them myself."

"I suppose," Jackson said bitingly, "you figure on selling my own notes back to me at a profit."

"Why don't you go along?" Serena suggested. "I'll come up to Pine Meadow and be there when the others come to talk in the morning."

Jackson's hand began to close on her wrist. The thick fingernails dug into her skin. She held herself tensely, staring at him. His face, yellow-brown below the leather-dark hair, was as grim as one of those Mexican faces carved in obsidian. She felt the skin cutting under his nails, and bit her lip to suppress a gasp. Jackson dropped her hand. He juggled the rifle and suddenly strode to the door.

"You'll find pants in my closet and plenty of straight razors. Maybe you'd like to add them to your wardrobe. But understand this. Neither you nor Cameron nor anybody else will get in my way without getting hurt."

When he slammed the front door, earth sifted from the willow boards above the ceiling beams. Serena rubbed the bluish crescents on her wrists. She was frightened and confused. A time she had loved very much was over. She felt as though she no longer knew her father, almost as though she scarcely knew herself. She wanted Troy terribly, to tell her it was going to be all right. But he was probably with that Becket girl at this very moment. In a flash of jealous anger, she flung her napkin on the table and left the room. *If she tries to take him away from me by flashing a red dress at him,* she thought, *she'll wish she'd've stayed in Texas.*

IX

"Do you always carry so many guns?" Frances Becket asked.

She smiled at Troy as the horses moved upward along the wagon road. They had started early with the girl's suitcase and some provisions loaded on a pack mule. It was still only midmorning, and the foothill air was sweet, clean, and soft. Among small cedars clustered with blue-gray berries were patches of reddish earth. There was a rifle under Troy's knee, and he carried a plain Colt.

"Might get an antelope," he said.

"But that's with the rifle. What's the revolver for?"

"In case I don't get him with the rifle."

"May I see it?"

"Just a forty-five-caliber Colt. Hogleg, some call them." But he handed it to her. "Now, don't say they don't carry them in Fort Worth, because I've been there."

He saw her peering at the handle of the revolver.

"No notches," he observed.

Her face tipped up. The strong sunlight found no flaws there.

She looked wonderfully healthy and rode her sidesaddle with supple ease.

"Gil told me you'd been a town marshal," she said. "I was sure there'd be notches."

"Bad advertising. Some fellow's always trying to see whether you were good enough to warrant the notches."

"Why did you quit to become a cowboy?"

Pushing the Colt back into the holster, Troy frowned. "Everybody asks that. I ran out of luck. That's all."

"Do you mean it was luck that you weren't afraid to face a gunman, and use your gun if you had to?"

"The most important thing about luck," Troy told her, "is thinking you have it. I got to thinking I didn't. Then a bullet clipped me, so I knew I didn't. That was when I quit."

She looked disappointed. "I was sure it had to do with being haunted by the ghosts of ... of men you'd ..." She hesitated delicately.

Troy smiled. "The only ghost that haunted me was the ghost of a man who was going to draw his gun first."

A short time later he heard team bells, and, without explaining to Frances, he swung out on a detour. From a hillside they looked down on a string of wagons and trailers and the broad backs of oxen. Earlier they had passed the spot at Sheep Bridge where Red Roth had camped the night before. He would camp again tonight and be in Pine Meadow early tomorrow.

"What are all those wagons?" Fran asked curiously.

"They're loggers' wagons. Man named Roth figures to cut some timber up here."

"How nice. That will mean extra money for the ranchers, won't it?"

Troy's gloved hand tugged the mule along. "Miss Frances, you just don't know a lot about this country, do you?"

Her face altered, offended, a little haughty. "Only what Gil—"

"Red Roth," Troy said, "works for Big Jim Jackson. Jackson has a halfway legal rope around folks' necks up here. Nobody's said he could, but he's cutting timber anyway. That's if something can't be worked out with him."

She took time to think. The horses gained a windy divide. Before them lay a canyon and then a series of soaring ridges fading west.

"Well, my goodness," she said, "this is the country of direct action, isn't it? Why doesn't someone take direct action against him?"

Troy led down the narrow trail that threaded a conglomerate of Spanish bayonet and ironwood, juniper, and pine. "I was taking direct action against Jackson yesterday when your stage came in. Even if you hadn't broken it up, I don't think I'd have worked anything out with him. I don't know … maybe he'll be able to foreclose all this land that he used to lease."

"I'm sure Gil and his friends will think of something," said Fran quietly. Then with a woman's directness she pointed out: "If you're really serious about Serena Jackson, it must make quite a difficult situation for you."

"Practically impossible," he agreed.

He gazed across the canyon. Something had taken his eye there. On that cold northern flank the sun never touched during the winter. The growth was heavy and dark green. Troy halted his horse in the thin sunlight and it squealed under the bit. He put out his hand to warn Fran. Then he saw the wink of flame.

"Get off!" he shouted, twisting, pulling at his rifle as he sprawled from the horse and started back to the girl. But she was smiling.

"If you'd rather not talk about her," she said, "you don't have to be so dramatic."

The bullet smashed into the ground near them and screamed away. A moment later the crash of the rifle reached them. Troy dragged the girl from the horse and thrust her behind a boulder. He ran forward a short distance and took shelter. Another bullet exploded in the rubble and shrieked over Troy's head. The horses began to run down the trail. Fran's pony squeezed between the pack mule and the hillside and the mule lost footing and started rolling down the slope.

There was nothing to fire at but a drifting blur of smoke. Troy laid the rifle barrel on the rock and waited. He saw the flash, then, and fired at it. Fran was calling to him.

"Troy! Troy! What's the matter?"

"Stay down!" Troy called back. The horses were still running. The pack mule had come to rest against a tree. Its packs were gone but the tarpaulin was still wrapped about it. Badly hurt, the mule kept raising and lowering its head. Troy took a bead on the animal's head and shot it. Across the canyon echoed an avalanche of their own jumbled voices, and shots.

"I'm coming down!" Fran cried.

"No!" He turned swiftly. He saw her rise and come down the trail, holding her skirts high. He swung back and commenced firing across the canyon to cover her. She dropped and huddled against him. His firing pin fell on a dead shell. Troy levered out this last cartridge and reloaded. Across the canyon it was still. The smoke had cleared from the dark growth, and now, faintly, he heard a horse traveling over rocks in some side canyon. Numbly he patted the girl's hand.

"Winter comes to the Defiances," he said.

Big-eyed, frightened but self-conscious, she moved away from him. "Was that ... was it a joke?"

He squinted one eye. "More than likely," he said, "it was direct action on somebody's part. We don't have time for jokes up here."

Although he did not mention Tom Doyle, he thought of him as they went on. Doyle had not been in town yesterday. Was he waiting out here in the hills? But why should he? Doyle was the kind of killer who liked an audience. Nevertheless Jim Jackson's hand was in it. He would bet on that.

* * * * *

Gil's place on Cave Creek was three miles past Mike Saddler's Pine Meadow ranch. Saddler had left Frontera the night before to check on his men before returning to the roundup. But no one was around when they reached Saddler's cabin and they rode on. Around midday they reached Gil's home place. Lying below the spine of the Defiances, his cabin and an awkward sprawl of sheds and corrals were half hidden among the pines. Gil had cleared some timber for pasture and built a structure of blackish stone against a slope. In the lean-to a sheet-iron stove with a rusting stovepipe could be seen. The stovepipe joined the chimney from the fireplace. Some Dutch ovens hung from hooks thrust into the stones. Hides lay across corral fences. The whole layout resembled an unkempt bedroom.

Suddenly he was ashamed of having let her think he worked for Gil—that boy wonder of the Defiances. But she had asked for it, with her talk of recalcitrant employees, and of firing him.

"Who owns this place?" Fran asked wearily, gazing at the buildings. They had not spoken much since the ambush. She was tired from the long ride, and upset.

Frowning fixedly at a broken bar of a corral, Troy said: "This is Gil's. A little rough, but it's snug."

"You mean it's his bunkhouse or something?"

"No," he said slowly, "it's his home place. This is it."

She made absolutely no sound. After an instant he looked up at her. She was going to weep. There was simply no question about that. She was tired and lonely and scared, and she was going to square with the world by weeping.

"I'm sorry," he said quickly. "I'd have told you, but it seemed like you were always telling me. Gil's getting on as well as anybody. But nobody but Mike Saddler has more than one cowpuncher up here. We sort of team up. You might say I was Gil's employee when he wasn't mine."

"You let me make a fool of myself," she said.

"I didn't mean to. It was kind of a joke. Not a very good one. I'm sorry, Miss Frances."

Her weeping was tight and silent and he wanted to suggest that she get it out of her system. "I'll tell you what," he said. "There's a cabin near where we're finishing the roundup. You'd be fairly comfortable there until you decide what you want to do."

"I'm going to … stay … of course," she whispered.

"Now, look," he said, "women don't stay alone in these hills. We'll rest the horses and go on."

She dismounted angrily, waving him away when he wanted to help. She was almost too stiff to walk. She began untying the bundle of things salvaged from the packs, which Troy had tied behind her saddle. Troy guiltily carried in her carpetbag that he had carried on his saddle. He heard a thud, and looked back to see that a burlap sack of provisions had dropped to the ground when she tried to lift it down. But when he hurried back, she straightened with tear-filled eyes.

"Don't touch it! I'd rather it rotted there than be helped by you."

"Now, Miss Frances." Troy smiled. She was so young and sweet and tired that he held both her arms and made her look at him. But he did not know what to say.

"When you go down," she said, "will you tell my brother I'm here?"

"It's going to be dark in a few hours. There aren't enough cartridges in Arizona for you to shoot at every sound you hear. You'd better come with me."

She pushed off his hands and walked to the doorway of the ranch house. "Thank you. I'll be all right. Good bye, Troy Cameron. Do you think I'll become a legend after you tell them? *The girl with the red dress and big ideas?*"

She went inside. Troy set everything beside the door, piled wood in the cooking lean-to, and finally placed his rifle, loaded and with his shell belt coiled about it, just inside the door.

"Adios," he said. In the cold cabin he could hear her crying.

X

Troy turned his jacket collar up as he approached the roundup camp on Muddy Creek. Dusk was near, his face was stiff with the mountain cold, and a warped cigarette, long dead, dangled from his lips as he jogged into camp. The smoke and supper smells began to restore him. Slack in the saddle, he swung off and saw Gil Becket coming to the picket line. He looked troubled and embarrassed.

"Lemme get that," Gil said hurriedly as Troy started to unsaddle.

Troy leaned against the horse and said: "Your sister's here, Gil."

"Mike told me. How ... how'd she take it?"

"Rough," Troy said. "You know, boss, you haven't paid me for nearly six months now. How about it?"

Gil's face reddened. "Well, I had to tell her something."

"You didn't have to tell her you were the Baron of Arizona. When I told her that was the home place, she busted out crying."

Gil turned away, driving one fist against his palm. "I'd have told you, if I'd've known she was coming. If I'd gotten to her first, I could have fixed everything up."

"With what ... some more tall ones? You'd better get up there, Gil. Even the coyotes go around in pairs up there at night. And after ..." He hesitated. Tempers were thin enough already, without word of the ambush. But it had to come out, if only to put everyone on guard. "Somebody took a couple of shots at us," he said.

Gil turned blankly. "Who?"

"Didn't see him."

Gil started back through the camp. Mike Saddler, Colonel Edwards, and the others were eating in silence near a fire.

"Hey," Gil called, "Jackson took a shot at Troy and my sis today!"

Troy walked into the warm surge of the fire. "I didn't say that," he reminded Gil. "I said somebody."

"That still spells Jackson," Gil retorted. "Look what he and Doyle done to Mike."

Seated against a log, Saddler gazed up at Troy. His florid features had a bee-stung look—both eyes puffed, his upper lip protruding. He stared at the tall man by the fire.

"What happened?" Troy asked him.

"Jackson and Doyle jumped me near Anvil turnoff," Saddler said. "Jackson roped me and then they both went after me."

Troy regarded him thoughtfully. It did not sound like Jim Jackson. But neither did the morning's ambush sound like Big Jim, or the encounter with him in the Pima Bar yesterday. Perhaps Jackson, faced with bankruptcy, had deliberately turned a corner.

"When was this?" he asked Saddler.

"Yesterday afternoon. I went up to my place after I came to. I told Bill Thorne and the Basque to shoot anybody that came onto the land."

"Getting a little ahead of yourself, aren't you, Mike?" Troy asked.

Saddler got up. Color surged into his face as he took hold of Troy's arm.

"I'll get my preachin' in church after this, deacon. I saw Jackson back you down in the saloon. I saw you go running after him when it was too late. OK. If you want to stand still till he chops you down, don't let me stop you. But nobody's speaking for Mike Saddler from here on out."

Colonel Edwards came between them, shoving Saddler back. "We hang together, Mike, or Jackson hangs us separate."

Saddler cuffed his hand away. "That's fine, Colonel. But not with Cameron making policy for us. When Roth's wagons roll into Pine Meadow tomorrow, I'm going to be waiting for them."

He walked to where his blankets and gear lay against a tree.

"You can't buck them alone," Troy warned.

Saddler straightened. "Reckon that's where you sing tenor and I sing bass. I figure nobody's any bigger than a man who won't be crowded."

While Saddler girthed up, the colonel talked quietly with Troy. "What about it? Any use going slow with Jackson now?"

"It's going to be a lot harder," Gil pointed out, "to throw him off than to keep him off."

"All I want," Troy said, "is to get a cease and desist before the shooting starts. That might take a week."

Saddler threw cross bucks onto a pack horse, loaded his war sack onto the animal, and swung into his saddle. He rode from the firelight. A moment later they heard his horses crossing the stream.

Troy got a plate of food. As he ate, he thought of his small ranch high in the mountains. He loved this ranching life, the feeling of being suspended between earth and blue sky, part of each. The life had grace and beauty. There was something beautiful, even, in the weary clutter of the roundup camp, in the sear and smoke of a brand laid black on a red hide. In the lonely stillness of Defiance Mountain it was hard to remember that he had once made his living tracking down scared men with a gun.

Finished with his food, he stood up. "If anybody wants to go with Mike, go ahead. I've been wrong before."

No one left. Still, as darkness closed, his mind rode with Saddler, going up to make his fight alone. If Mike bulled into it and got himself killed, he would have it on his conscience forever.

* * * * *

The cold awakened him. Needle-sharp, it had settled into the canyon. He lay, trying to rouse himself to get a horse blanket to throw over his bedroll. But then his mind was on Saddler and Fran Becket again. But, of course, no one would bother the girl. He sat up and rolled a cigarette. Saddler was the real worry. With his rashness, he would probably get himself shot or shoot someone else.

In the darkness, Gil spoke nervously: "I wish I'd gone up there, tonight. She'll be scared stiff."

"I told you that. And that jughead, Saddler," Troy muttered.

"Still," said Colonel Isaac Edwards from his blankets, "he's one of the bunch."

A rancher named Bob Briscoe spoke: "We never should have let him go. We came here together. We should stay together."

"Mike quit the bunch," Troy said. "The bunch didn't quit him. I know what you mean, though. We could leave Gil with his sister and make Mike's place by sunup."

"Damn my aching bones," the colonel groaned.

More men were sleepily sitting up. Colonel Edwards rose from his blankets, underwear-clad. He threw some brush on the fire. It smoked and blazed up.

"You're wearing the badge, Colonel," Troy said. "You and your aching bones will have to lead the parade. Let's go."

The colonel selected Gil, Bob Briscoe, and two other men in addition whose ranches were near Saddler's A-Bar to accompany them. They saddled in the darkness. In the darkness they rode out. The horses worked hard in the cold, climbing a ridge and descending into a valley to leave Muddy Creek behind. High and far, a lobo howled.

The trail swept southwest, climbing, descending, climbing. The mountain chain—this sheer-walled island of timber in the desert—formed a long arm running north and south. They reached West Rim, a few hundred feet above the lonely high-country flats where Troy had his Government Springs Ranch. He had not seen his place in two weeks. He was homesick for the cluttered cabin and the long timbered bench.

Suddenly the colonel clutched his arm. "Moses and Aaron!" he exclaimed. "That there's a fire!"

He had been riding ahead of Troy and had seen it first. There was a clutch at Troy's heart like a muscular cramp, a hard grip of shock, and then a slackness. The colonel was wrong. It had been a fire. It had been a cabin, too, but now it was a puddle of coals.

Along the rim the horsemen lined up, gazing down at it. The wind, sweeping from the desert, was fragrant with smoke. The colonel looked around at them.

"Man, this is a long way from Mike's place. If Jackson burned your cabin, Troy, it stands to reason he burned Mike's and Gil's on the way …"

Troy thought of the frightened girl spending her first night alone in the mountains. Without warning, Gil pulled out of line and started south on the trail to Cave Creek. The others followed.

The night was beginning to wear out when they came to the foot of the horse pasture in the gray cold. Long arms of timber reached into the pasture, and beyond. Troy could see the bulwarks of rock on the hillside above the sheds and corrals.

"Well, there it is," Gil said.

The cabin had been set afire more recently, but only one wall remained. Gil loped up the meadow. As they rode into the yard, the girl appeared from the brush. Troy watched Gil embrace the girl and saw Fran's face in the firelight, pallid and strained. And he wished by every tree in the mountains that he had not brought her up here.

"Did you see anybody?" Gil was asking her.

"Three men," she said. "Something woke me and I looked out and saw three men riding away. The lean-to was already burning."

"Jackson, Doyle, and Roth," Gil said bitterly. "Get some things together, Sis. We'll take you on to Mike Saddler's and you can stay there."

Once, as they rode on, Troy pulled in beside the girl. "It's a big order ... but can you forgive me?" he asked.

A fresh amber light was spreading over the mountain slopes. Fran gazed ahead. "If there's anyone to forgive, it's myself. For ever coming here."

Saddler's headquarters, at the upper end of Pine Meadow, overlooked six miles of grass between fringes of blue timber. In the early dawn it was beautiful and still. Far down the meadow gleamed a large pond with a mill and race at the end of it. Among the near trees they could see smoke. Nobody was surprised to find Mike Saddler sitting on a boulder near the smoking shell of his cabin, a rifle across his knees. Wiley, his Basque cowpuncher, was drawing a cleaning rag through a carbine, and Bill Thorne, hands on hips, stood with his back to the newcomers, gazing at the cabin.

Saddler returned Troy's stare. "What's the matter?" he jeered. "Ain't you ever seen a man burned out before?"

"Sure," Troy said. "They burned Gil and me out, too."

Saddler looked down at the gun and rubbed the bronze frame of it with his sleeve.

"Did you save anything?" Troy asked.

"Yeah." Saddler glanced up as if he had heard something in Troy's tone that offended him. "We saved one butter mold, that jackleg table yonder, and ourselves ... just as the roof caved in. I got here about eight, and the fun started around the time I got to sleep." He swore. "Help yourselves to grain for your horses, boys," he said. "Plenty in the grain shed. Only they dumped lime in it."

"See any of them?" Gil asked.

"Jackson and Doyle. We scouted down to the mill. They must've spent part of the night there after they finished their fun. Then we rode up to the ridge. There's wagons coming up the grade." Saddler called sharply to Joe Wiley: "Get done with honing that meat-getter! I mean to hit 'em where the road's narrowest. That's just below the pass, and about where they ought to be right now."

He got up abruptly, slapped his hand over his rifle, and headed for a corral where his pony stood saddled. Colonel Edwards nodded at Troy. "Throw in with 'im?"

Killing was serious business. It bothered Troy that they did not know for sure that Jackson had burned them out. He glanced at Joe Wiley, the dark-faced cowboy he had never warmed to. Wiley was smiling to himself.

"I suppose so," he said. "But let's do it without shooting." He heard Gil talking to Fran as he helped her to the ground.

" ... They won't bother you here. You've got Troy's carbine if you see anybody."

The girl looked taut enough to snap like a wire. Awkwardly she held the gun Gil thrust at her. Full of enthusiasm and immature fight, Gil turned back to the others. *You damned little fool,* Troy thought. *Throw a gun at her and leave her alone!* Then, to his surprise, she turned helplessly to him.

"Troy?" she said. He rode over. "Do look out for him, please," she said. "He's so young ... so foolish. Don't let him get hurt."

"No one's going to get hurt," Troy promised. "We're going to hit those bull teams and spill them down the canyon. We're sort of returning the compliment, you see."

"I know. But if anything happened to him now ..."

"I'll stay with him. If I were you, I'd ride back in the trees and stay out of sight."

From Saddler's cabin a trail slanted up to a ridge. After following the ridge two miles, they reached a saddle through which Jackson's old wagon road came to Pine Meadow. They turned back down the slope toward the meadow until they were just above the little sawmill Jackson had built years ago. Three horses stood by the pond. Two men were walking toward them—Tom Doyle and Jim Jackson. The range was about two hundred yards.

"We've got to hold them here," Troy declared. "If they reach it to the wagons at the time we do, things might get tough."

Saddler drew his carbine. "There were only two ponies down there before. Maybe Roth came up ahead of his wagons. OK, let's hold 'em here. They won't travel fast without horses." He set the gun against his shoulder.

Troy slapped the rifle barrel aside. "Wait!" he snapped. "There's a girl down there!"

He had just seen her coming from the cabin, a girl with black hair shining in the morning sun. Serena walked among the horses to pick up the reins of a long-legged black. He saw Jackson help her into the saddle.

"She's Jackson's worry," Saddler growled.

"If you raise that rifle ...," Troy warned.

"Who's raising it?" Saddler retorted, winking at the others. "If we can't handle them here, we can handle them across the ridge."

He sent his pony lunging up the hillside. Gil caught the fight fever and whipped his horse with his hat as he tried to catch up with him. Even the colonel strung along. They crossed the ridge and rode through brush for a mile before coming in sight of the wagon road. It lay below them, angling steeply along the mountainside. Troy heard the bronze jingling of team bells. Gil and the others gathered about Saddler.

"The first wagons are carrying the supplies," the rancher told them. "The log trailers come last. A man to a wagon ought to swing it. Hit 'em hard, flog the teams over, and keep riding. We'll meet at Sheep Bridge and head back to camp." He paused. "There comes Jackson and his filly," he said.

Jim Jackson jogged down the road behind his daughter. His big jaw was set. Troy had the impression that Jackson was starting the girl home—that she had come up without permission and he had taken her in hand. Behind the cowman rode Tom Doyle, short and strong, his hat pulled down, his coat collar turned up. He slipped a bottle from his coat, drew the cork with his teeth, and took a drink.

The trio rode out of sight.

"Now, we wait," Saddler said through his teeth. He glanced along the line of horsemen in the brush. The road was fifty feet below. They waited. The first bull team appeared, heads low and swinging. Wooden axles squealed. A horseman swerved around the ox team and took his place at the head of the train. Tom Doyle had come back.

XI

Another wagon passed, but there was no sign of Serena or Jackson. Saddler tugged the brim of his sombrero down like a man about to step into the wind.

"Are we straight on it?" he asked. "A man to a wagon. Slug any 'whacker that makes trouble. Cameron, maybe you'd better get back with the women and kids. This is going to be all fight, no talk."

"Fine," Troy said. "I'll take Doyle. Unless you'd counted on him."

Saddler looked surprised. "He's yours," he said.

Troy had planned to keep Gil with him, but as Saddler spurred down the hill, Gil went with the rancher. Troy started down. He saw a dozen gaunt wagons. One wagon was filled with workmen. He slanted down the hillside until he was just above Doyle. The gunman was rolling a cigarette. Troy hit the road and spurred up behind him. Just then the teamster in back of him bawled: "Doyle! Behind you!"

Doyle dropped his tobacco and his body wrenched around. He had the reflexes of an animal. His hand swept to his gun as Troy swung at his head. He pulled the gun clear but the bullet blasted into the ground. Troy piled onto the gunman and they fell and landed on the hillside. Doyle's gun got lost as they began rolling. Troy hung on and tried to get a blow at his chin, but holding Doyle was like wrestling a pig. Doyle was muscular and thick-bodied and he fought viciously.

They struck a boulder and sprawled apart. Up on the road bull-whackers were shouting and a wagon went over with a splintering crash. He heard a shot, heard Saddler bawling like a cavalry sergeant. Then he saw Doyle coming up and went after him. Doyle got set and threw a roundhouse swing at his head. Troy went under it and smashed Doyle hard on the chin. The gunman sat down. Above them another wagon toppled among the rocks and a man bawled in terror. Tom Doyle came up, dazed but stubborn. Troy went in grimly, a long dusty man with blood on his face. He sank his fist in Doyle's belly and whipped an uppercut to his chin that tipped the gunman's face up. Doyle fell straight back. He lay on the slope with one leg twisted under him.

A shot cracked nastily. Then there were more reports and a long screaming ricochet. Troy could see nothing for dust. He remembered his promise to Fran to watch out for Gil, and hoped she could not hear the shots. A man shouted: "Git, boys! Git!" It sounded like the colonel.

Troy ran for his horse. He rode through the dust, trying to follow the running horses in a giant confusion of crates, wagon wheels, and dazed teamsters. Ahead of him a bay horse was trying to run. Its rider had fallen, but the man's boot had caught in the stirrup. Troy caught the animal by the reins and held it while he worked the rider's boot from the stirrup. The horse went pitching into the woods and Troy knelt by the man.

Vaguely he remembered the fat cheeks like a squirrel's, the receding chin and heavy-lidded eyes. Roth had called him Deke. His eyes were open but filming. There was a deep wound in his neck but the blood had stopped pumping from it.

A horse was galloping on the road. Troy dashed to his horse and cut downward through the trees after the others. After he covered a couple of hundred feet, he came upon a downed horse trying to rise. A short distance beyond he heard a man running. It was Gil. He spurred up to him and Gil pivoted and swung a Colt. Troy scarcely knew the scared features.

Gil began babbling the story. "Never shot that fellow, Troy. I was firing at the ground, trying to scare him …"

As the horse moved on, Troy asked sharply: "Did you kill him? You ought to know."

"I don't know, Troy! Honest to God! He began shooting at me and Mike and Joe Wiley, and he hit my horse. We all shot back and he dropped."

"Where's your carbine?"

"Lost it. When my horse went down."

Among the trees, Troy saw the horse that the logger had been riding. It had stopped in a thicket. They moved in on it and Gil caught the bridle and scrambled into the saddle. As they left the thicket, a rider came through some junipers above them and halted. Gil's gun was already shakily lining out. With an oath, Troy knocked his arm down.

"It's Serena Jackson! Now, straighten out. Put that thing away."

He rode to meet the girl. "Troy!" she cried. "What is it? What's happened?"

"I'm not sure. But a man was hurt."

Troy saw her eyes fill.

"Why did you do it? Didn't you know what would happen?"

"We thought we could do it without any fuss," he said. "Just a quick raid and we'd take off. Serena, I've got to get Gil out of here. His horse and gun are back there. Roth will be after him with a rope."

"It won't do any good to get him out of the mountains. Dad will find him wherever he goes."

"If we can get him to town, though …"

"Do you think they won't find him there?" Serena said. "He can't hide in someone's home, and Dad will go through every store in town. And of course if Gil's killed a man, he'll have to pay for it."

"Yes ... after he's been tried. But I never was much for lynch law."

"Nor am I." She frowned, then brightened. "Do you know where I'd go, if I were Gil? To Fred Stiles' church."

"Churches have been searched before."

"But this church," she said, "has a belfry which has been boarded up for months. You see, I gave Reverend Stiles a bell. He's kept it as a surprise for his first service. Gil could hide there. I don't think it would occur to anyone."

Troy drew a deep breath. He took her face between his hands.

"You're a good girl," he said. "You're as smart as any two men I know."

She closed her eyes, and he kissed her. He felt her trembling. He wanted to say everything was going to come out all right, but she knew as well as he that something good had ended and that the new thing that had started would change them all.

Her eyes opened and she tried to smile. "Smart?" she asked. "Is that all? What girl wants to be smart?"

"Smart," he said, "and beautiful, and wonderful on top of that."

"Now," she said, sitting back, "you can go on."

Suddenly he remembered Fran Becket. Not far away men were shouting. Jim Jackson would be coming along soon. "Will you do one other thing? Gil's sister is at Saddler's. Three of us were burned out last night and we left her there. Will you take her to town with you?"

She smiled slightly. "It's an odd request, you know. I hope you're asking the favor for Gil and not yourself."

"It's for the girl. This has been pretty rough for her."

"I know. Tell Gil she'll be all right."

"I said you were a good girl." Troy smiled. "Now, if you'd just tell your father you saw Gil and me swap horses, I think he'd have a chance. If they take off after anybody, it will be me."

* * * * *

Three miles from where they had attacked the wagons, Mike Saddler and the others drew up by Sheep Bridge where the wagon road crossed Muddy Creek. Saddler glanced at Joe Wiley and closed one eye. Bill Thorne wiped his mouth with his sleeve and Saddler wondered which one of them had killed Deke Howard, the logger. Because he knew he hadn't and it didn't seem likely that Gil could have hit him with a Colt at that range.

In Saddler there was a gusty turmoil. It had all happened so fast and so satisfactorily, so much better than he could have hoped. They heard horses running, and squared away for trouble. But it was Troy Cameron and Gil who came in. They checked their mounts beside the old log bridge.

Colonel Edwards slid off his horse. The old man looked really done, Saddler thought—his face pocketed with exhaustion, lips thinned back from long yellow teeth, the white stubble on his chin and cheeks like frost. Numbly chafing his hands together, he stared out over the foothills.

"Man, man, I've got the weak trembles for sure," he panted. "I've really got 'em this time."

"We'd better split up," Bob Briscoe was saying. "Give them more trails to follow."

"Split up!" Saddler snorted. "If Gil's got any chance at all, it's by all of us staying together."

"Me!" Gil exclaimed. "Why me?"

"Because they'll find your horse! And you lost your damned carbine, too. Who do you think they'll come after?"

"But I never shot that fellow, Mike," Gil argued. "I was firing at the ground. I just …"

"You jughead," Saddler said with a sour grin. "You got a ricochet! Next time fire over a man's head. My God, I'd think you'd know that."

Saddler did not know for sure who had shot that logger. He did not care. But looking around at the exhausted men, he knew one thing. They were with him now. He had given them a crusade by burning their cabins. He had given Jackson a crusade by raiding the wagons. Jackson could no longer fight Mike Saddler without taking on every man in the Defiances.

What happened now would depend on Jackson. But there was no doubt that he would have to see Gil punished to keep Roth around. And if anything happened to Gil, the war would be on for sure.

"Get aboard, cowboy," Saddler told Gil shortly. "We've got tracks to make."

Cameron had not spoken since he and Gil pulled in. "Where to?" he asked.

"To camp. We can't go much farther on these animals."

"Gil can. He's riding a fresh one. The rest of us ought to split up to give them more trails to follow."

"I'd hate like hell," Saddler scoffed, "to be Gil, and riding Deke Howard's horse when they caught up."

"I told Serena to tell them we'd swapped horses. So when they come in sight of me, they'll think they're after Gil. That'll give him time to make it to Frontera." He looked at Gil for approval. But Gil, biting his lip, only stared at him.

Saddler interposed his cold-jawed will harshly. "What happens in Frontera? Does he stand them off in the Pima Bar?"

"He knows what to do when he gets there."

"But his friends," Saddler said sarcastically, "can't be trusted to know where he is, eh?"

"Fewer that knows," the colonel snapped, "fewer that'll spill it. Git ridin', Becket! Fellers die settin' still."

Once more Gil tried to explain how the logger had been shot, but everyone seemed too played out to pay attention to him. Saddler felt fresh and strong and excited. He quirted Gil's pony, and Gil grabbed the horn and crossed the bridge. Old Colonel Edwards, waving his arm, cried: "Split up, now! But everybody be at the Pima Bar tonight! I'm setting them up for the whole crowd."

They clattered across the bridge and broke up. As Saddler rode on, he saw Cameron lazily drawing his saddle girth up a notch, and he thought: *What a hell of a chance to take for a runt of the litter like Becket. Roth will skin him out like a muskrat if he catches him.*

XII

Troy smoked a cigarette as he waited by the bridge. It was very quiet. Camp-robber jays scolded from the junipers. Done in, his pony stood with hung head. He thought glumly of Gil's sister receiving the news that Gil was on the dodge. It would chill her on the whole territory, and on him particularly for not keeping Gil out of trouble. It concerned him that she should be angry with him. At first he had thought her spoiled and haughty, but he realized that inexperience instead had been her big trouble. She was getting plenty of experience now. Well, she was young, but either she would be a lot older soon or she would break down.

High in the timber above Muddy Creek he heard the horses coming.

Troy threw the cigarette in the stream. Mounted, he waited for them to descend the slope. They stopped and examined the tracks once. When the trail joined the wagon road, they came on rapidly. He waited until he could see them. There were about eight, he figured, coming with drawn rifles down the road. Troy hit his pony with the spurs.

The horse clattered over the bridge and a moment later someone shouted, and then he heard a bullet smack a tree behind him. He put his weight on the stirrups and leaned forward, making it easy on the tired horse, but it ran unevenly. He left the road and crashed through a thicket. Glancing back, he saw Jackson, big and solid on his horse, and Roth riding hatless behind him. A narrow gully opened before him. He gave the pony the spurs and tried to lift it into a jump. He felt the horse gather itself. Then without warning it stopped, forelegs braced, and he smashed into the saddle horn, lost his stirrups, and went over the animal's head.

He saw the sandy bed of the gully beneath him and was trying to decide whether to cushion his fall with his hands when he landed.

He heard a voice like that of a baying hound. He moved slowly on the sand. With a rush it came back to him. He tried to get up, but he was too hurt to move fast, and, as he crouched there, he saw the horsemen line up, one after the other, on the bank of the gully. Jackson and Roth, Tom Doyle and some other riders. Jackson's big, square face with his auburn mustaches was stony.

"Damn it," he said, "it's Cameron."

Red Roth, the roany-haired, gristly little woodsman, slid into the gully. He wrenched Troy's Colt from the holster and thrust it under his belt. Then he twisted Troy's arm up between his shoulder blades. "Which way, Cameron?" he asked.

Troy slugged at Roth's face. He hit one of the vein-shot cheek bones, and the man stumbled back. Roth pulled his Colt, but Jackson's voice came down like a club.

"Red, you damned little grease ant! We're looking for Becket!"

Roth straightened and spat. "Make him talk, then."

Troy rose. Jackson began talking hard and forcefully to him. "We've got him like a fly in a bottle, Cameron. If he tries to cross the desert or holes up in the mountains, I'll smoke him out in two days. If he hides in Frontera, I know every back room and alley in that town."

"What will you guarantee him if he turns himself in?" Troy asked.

"He'll get a trial. That's all I'll guarantee, though."

"Why, sure," Roth said, grinning. "I've got a white wig I wear when I try bushwhackers. Only trial he'll get is a high limb and a low horse."

Jackson scowled. "Shut up, Red. We'll talk about that when we get him. What about it, mister?" he asked Troy. "Does he turn himself in?"

"Not while Roth's in the deal. There seems to be a little confusion about guarantees."

"But there's no confusion about my finding him," Jackson retorted. "Red, take him up to where you camped last night. I'll stay on Becket's trail and send word back later if I don't find him. I'll be taking Frontera apart tonight if I don't. If you change Mister Cameron's mind, I'll be in town."

After Jackson and his posse left, Roth and a gaunt woodsman with cheek bones like stones tied Troy's ankles together under his horse and took him back to the road. A mile beyond Sheep Bridge they came to the place where Roth's outfit had camped. There was a litter of trash and trampled earth here; a few trees had been felled to make a bullpen. Roth sat his buckskin pony beside Troy's while he looked the area over, humming to himself and twirling the end of a rope.

"Hey!" the gaunt man said. He spoke a language that was more Scandinavian than English, and Roth called him Swede. "That there barber chair!" Hasty felling had caused a massive splinter to remain standing, high and jagged, like a chair back fixed to the stump. Swede led Troy's horse to the stump. Looking at the white, saber-like splinters, Troy felt panic. The logger dragged him from the horse. Then he struck him in the face. When he reeled against the stump, Swede threw a rope over him. He slipped behind the stump and the rope went tight.

Roth skeptically picked his teeth. "I hope you aren't thinking of starvation, because that's going to take time."

"Watch," Swede said. He found a branch two inches thick and snapped it off so that it was about the length of an ax helve. He went behind the stump and the rope tightened as he inserted it under the rope. Troy could see his shadow as he wound the branch around like a lever. The rope tightened like a wire guy in a fence. Troy gasped. Now he understood. Roth smiled with pleased comprehension.

"Yes, sir," he said. "A persuader. That's what we've got here. Cinch it up some more."

The rope bit into Troy's arms and chest so that he had to set his teeth against the pain.

"Where's Becket?" Roth asked, his filmy blue eyes intent.

"The hell with you," Troy said.

Roth nodded and the rope tightened. *My God,* Troy thought, *my God, it's going to cut me in two!* The blood was cut off in his arms. When he breathed, the pressure of the rope against his ribs was unbearable.

"Back off," Roth told his man, and the rope slackened. "Where is he?" Roth asked.

"Would you tell on one of your men?" Troy asked.

"No, but you're the fella in trouble, not me."

"All right, find him yourself."

Roth walked behind the stump and took the branch from the woodsman. He brought it around clock-hand fashion and the rope slapped Troy against the stump with the dead force of a bull hitting the end of a rope. He groaned. He felt his ribs being forced inward and a sharp pain crossed his chest. Roth made a quick bight with the rope, securing the lever, and walked around to peer into Troy's face. Troy closed his eyes.

"Cigarette?"

Roth seemed to have said it several times. He had rolled and lighted a cigarette and was offering it to Troy. Troy opened his lips. Roth broke the cigarette open and shook the tobacco on the ground.

"I reckon not." He smiled sadly. "I've heard it stunts a fella's growth. Wouldn't want to be accused of doin' that to a man. Swede," he said, "what time's it gettin' to be?"

The logger pulled out a thick watch. "One o'clock."

"Day's goin' fast," Roth commented. "Let's take a ride up yonder and see how they're gettin' on with the cleanup. We'll be back in an hour or so," he told Troy. "Anything you want to say before we go?"

Troy shut his eyes.

XIII

Fran heard the shots while she waited on a hillside near Mike Saddler's burned cabin. There among the trees it was cold, and she drew into the blanket she was wearing, chilled and frightened. She had not carried the gun to the rocks where she was hiding. She would not have had the wits to fire it even if she needed it.

Again she heard rifles, and then silence, and she prayed for Gil. Her mind was as disordered as an attic. Somewhere she heard a horse. She stood up to look down the long valley, but could not see the rider. Yet she still heard the hooves approaching. Saddler's cabin was a couple of hundred yards below, just beyond the trees. She hoped it would be Gil—or his friend, Troy Cameron. There was a dependability about Troy, a decency and a respect for others. He had asked her pardon for letting her make a fool of herself, and he seemed to mean it. She wished he were leading the raid against the wagons instead of that man Saddler.

Now she saw a rider come into Saddler's ranch yard and stop. It was neither Gil nor Troy. It was Serena Jackson. She started down the hill at once. Then she heard the girl calling her name.

"Frances! Frances Becket!"

Fran called back. "Wait for me!"

When she reached the ranch yard, she found Serena standing, looking at the burned cabin. She was really a beautiful girl, Fran thought. She was tiny, with a wonderful figure. Her hair was black and her complexion rich and smooth. Her eyes were gray-green, the color of junipers, and her face was fine, with perhaps just a little of the expression you would expect in the daughter of a wealthy man. Fran did not know what to say. Gil and his friends were out making war on her father at this moment. Did Serena know it?

Serena spoke crisply: "I'm to take you to town, Frances. Troy asked me to see that you got there safely."

"Troy? Have you seen him this morning?"

"Just a few minutes ago. There was some trouble, and since no one will be able to come back for you ..."

"My brother's been hurt?" Fran said.

"No, but someone else has. Where is your horse?"

"In the trees. Was it Troy?" Fran asked tensely.

Serena studied her with quiet curiosity. "No, it wasn't Troy," she said quietly. "Do you really think I'd be up here worrying about you if Troy were hurt?"

Fran felt a blush rising to her throat. "I ... I wasn't thinking." Then she added: "You haven't told me what happened."

"A logger was killed. We'd better be starting," Serena said impatiently. "Is there some food we can take? We're going to be late."

There was a small stone spring house at the side of a little stream that flowed past Saddler's buildings. "Perhaps in there," Fran said.

As they walked to the stone hut, Serena said: "I suppose you think my father is terrible for burning the cabins last night."

"Someone is terrible," Fran said.

"And of course it must be my father, since he's so handy to blame."

"I don't blame anyone, yet," Fran told her.

"But when you get around to blaming someone," Serena said, "of course it will be Big Jim."

"Miss Jackson," Fran said desperately, "I never saw the Defiance Mountains until the day before yesterday. I know there's bad feeling, but how can I form an opinion so quickly? And Troy tells me it can still be worked out."

"No," Serena said gravely, "not after today."

"But if the man who killed the logger is … is tried …"

"Frances," Serena said quickly, "I didn't want to tell you this. But they think Gil killed him."

Fran shut her eyes. She leaned against the spring house. Somehow she had known something like this had happened. "Where is he?"

"He's on his way to Frontera. He's to hide in the belfry of the church. He'll be all right until they can move him. I'm sorry," she said, "but Troy said I should tell you."

Fran could not speak. She worked at the latch of the spring house door. Inside, it was redolent of smoked hams and rancid butter. Serena pressed past her and began gathering a few things in her shawl.

"Mister Saddler," she said, "should churn his butter before the cream goes sour. Heavens."

Fran was thinking of Gil when he was a boy. He had dreamed more than most and his coming here when he was only twenty-one was scarcely more than a dream. He was no better prepared for ranching in a wilderness than she was.

"Look here!" Serena exclaimed. Fran peered into the gloomy stone hut. "A bullet mold. A clock. Two chairs and a tool chest. Isn't a spring house an odd place to store things like that?" She came out and stared at Fran. "I declare, he's put everything he owns in there!"

"But it's a shelter," Fran said. "Perhaps he saved them from the fire. No, that couldn't be." She remembered what Saddler had said about saving a butter mold and a table.

Serena's dark-lashed eyes watched her closely.

"So he must have moved them here before the fire," Fran concluded. Now she understood what it meant. "Why, if he moved them before the fire, it could have been Saddler who set the fire. Else how would he have known it was coming?"

Serena gazed down the meadow, her eyes bitter. "And because of him a man has been murdered."

"We must tell Troy," Fran insisted. "After everyone knows it, it will take the pressure from Gil. They may even find Saddler was guilty of the killing."

"Yes, it's nice to think so," Serena said coolly.

"Miss Jackson," Fran cried, "I'm trying to be fair! I haven't told you I'm frightened for Gil because you were the one who picked his hiding place. I haven't said anything about my brother and his friends being burned out. Can't you at least be as fair?" Serena smiled. "I haven't said I resented your traipsing around with my fiancé, either."

"I haven't been traipsing around with him," Fran protested. "Someone had to take me to Gil's cabin, and Troy was the only one who was there."

"I know. But I can't make myself believe it, somehow. That's the way your mind works when you love someone. You think of all the things you've meant to each other, of your kisses …"

"I'll get my horse," Fran said, turning away. She was obscurely piqued. It was no business of hers if Troy had kissed Serena. But she didn't like Serena throwing it up to her. *Well, why not?* she asked herself. *Am I jealous, too? Of a man I scarcely know?*

Serena was tying a small parcel of provisions to her saddle. Fran took the carpetbag Troy had had her bring. When she finished tying the roll to her saddle, she saw Serena watching her.

"Are you taking anything along for dress-up occasions?" the girl asked with a suggestion of a smile.

"If you mean that red dress," Fran flared, "I asked Troy to tell everyone how I really happened to have it. Didn't he tell you?"

"Yes." Serena smiled, but her smile said: *Who would believe such a tale?* "But I thought, in case you needed to impress anyone ..."

Fran slapped her. Serena gasped and touched her cheek. They stood staring at each other. Then Fran began to weep. She turned to mount. She heard Serena mounting, also. Finally she heard Serena say throatily: "Forgive me. I'll try to behave."

XIV

Once Troy tried to slide down the stump, but the bark gouged his back and the rope that bound him did not give. In desperation, he tried by lunging against it to gain slack. He heard the rope groan, but when he relaxed, sick and sweating with pain, Roth's lever arrangement recovered the slack.

He did not know how long Roth was gone. But suddenly he and Swede were back. Roth was pulling off buckskin gloves as he stood, spraddle-legged, before him.

"Man, you got to start taking care of yourself," Roth said in fake concern. "You're looking poorly. What've you got to say for yourself?"

Troy cursed him quietly. He was obsessed with Roth's brawl-marked face, with the broken nose and filmy eyes.

"Temper," Roth cautioned. "Reckon we ought to take up some more slack, Swede?"

The logger moved behind the stump. Roth stood there while Swede worked with the knot Roth had thrown over the branch.

"That fella's name was Deke Howard," Roth said sadly. "He

was with me eight years. Got a nice family. If I thought you'd shot him, I'd pull you right through that stump. Maybe I'll have to anyway. Ready?" he asked the logger, moving to the side of the stump to take the lever.

Swede said, "Take holt," and there was a sudden lessening of tension in the rope. A whistling sound cut the air. Swede gasped, "Look out!" and tried to catch the helve, but it went over like a semaphore. Troy saw Roth duck but the branch struck him on the side of the head. Dazed, he went heavily to his knees. It had all happened in a fraction of a second.

For an instant Troy stood there, feeling the hot rush of blood into his arms, and filling his lungs with air as cold and sweet as brook water. Swede was bending over Roth, who remained on his knees, stunned. He was telling him how it had happened.

Then Troy realized the rope had begun sliding down. He looked dumbly at it. It lay loosely about his waist. Quickly he drew up his arms, took hold of the rope, and pushed it down. He took one long, restorative breath, draining the strength from it. Then he moved quietly behind the logger and cocked his arm. Just as he threw the blow, Swede glanced around. Troy went forward with the swing, driving viciously at Swede's jaw. He jarred Swede's head and they went down in front of Red Roth. Troy scrambled on top of him and chopped at the logger's jaw until the man went slack.

He came up then, turning swiftly as Roth got on his feet. Roth had drawn his Colt. He was white, but his jaw was set and he was trying to point the gun. When it went off, the concussion jarred Troy like a door slammed in his face. Powder sparks stung his cheek. The bullet hit the stump behind him. He pushed himself at Roth and the gun. His hand took the gun barrel and twisted it. He raised it as Roth staggered aside. He chopped. Roth took the butt of the gun on the back of his head, stumbled, and fell.

Troy had to lean back against the stump. Everything glistened with the unnatural brightness that told a man he was going to faint.

He stood with his face tilted up, breathing deeply. At last he knelt by Roth and took his gun from Roth's belt. He walked drunkenly to his pony, grazing in the bullpen. He put it on the road to Frontera.

* * * * *

All afternoon Big Jim Jackson had marshaled the search through the foothills and over the broken desert. There were plenty of fresh trails to follow, but always someone like Bob Briscoe or old Colonel Ike turned up at the end of them, resting his horse or building himself a smoke. And you could not jail every man you encountered on the ground that he lived in the Defiances.

Late in the afternoon Roth rejoined him. He had a headache from a head blow that took a pint of whiskey to kill. At last Jackson, with sunset promising, took Roth, Doyle, his range boss Owen McCard, and four of his cowpunchers, leaving the others to watch the trails, and headed for Frontera. Darkness came before they reached the village.

In the windy night, they rode into Frontera. Along the streets, lamps shone with a hard desert glitter. Jackson heard Doyle humming to himself.

"What makes you so damned musical?" Jackson growled.

"Gonna see the bottom of Becket's boots before the sun rises," Doyle said cheerfully. "Gonna get me a grass rope, a little old tree, and set him on a horse."

"Dream on," Jackson scoffed. He was growing disgusted with this highly paid specialist of his. "What's Troy Cameron going to be doing all this time?" he baited Doyle.

Then he saw that Doyle, for all his grinning, was as grim as a cocked Colt. A stubble of blond whiskers made his mouth coarse, and with his bruised face and his hat tugged low he had a look of single-minded ugliness.

"It ain't a question of what Cameron's going to be doing

about me," Doyle said. "It's a question of how'll he have it ...
standing up or sitting down. That's all he's got to decide."

As they rode down the narrow slot of the business section,
Jim Jackson saw a woman herd a small boy into the doorway of
a store. He rode into Mundy's feed barn. Mundy was at the door
of his office.

"Seen Becket?" Jackson snapped.

Mundy stroked his soiled beard. "Reckon not, Jim."

"Don't Jim me, you old pirate!" Mundy had cornered half of
Jackson's beef money by threatening a lawsuit unless his feed bills
were paid up.

As they rode on, Jackson told Roth to ride a block north and
take the alley to the rear of the Pima Bar. "Doyle and I'll go in the
front. If he's in there, we've got him."

He had already seen the congregation of horses before the
saloon. As they continued, Jackson watched the stores and boardwalks, Doyle looked straight ahead, the other men crowded close,
hard jawed and silent.

There was no room at the Pima Bar hitch rack, and Jackson
shoved along until he found space. Doyle crowded in ahead of him
and slid off the back of his pony. As Jackson found another opening,
Doyle pulled up his belt, loosened his gun in the holster, and flexed
his fingers. "Yes, sir!" he said.

He cracked the door open with his knee and stood in the
opening. Jackson came up close behind him. "You're a hell of a fine
target," he prodded.

"Nobody in this tin-can town could hit a target," Doyle retorted.

Jackson put his hand on his shoulder. "Watch the door, now. I
want to smell around a bit."

Doyle started to protest, but Jackson sauntered into the room.
McCard and the other men moved with him and settled along the
bar, their backs to it. Men who had been drinking there quietly
drifted away. Jim Jackson inventoried the long room. Cameron,

Mike Saddler, and Colonel Ike Edwards sat at a table, and Nate Croft was bringing a tray bearing a bottle, some spiced Mexican meats, and a loaf of rye bread. At another table sat Joe Wiley, Saddler's Basque cowpuncher, and Bill Thorne. Wiley had the coloring of a bay horse, red brown skin and black hair, and his eyes were cold as ice on a pond. Other Defiance Mountains ranchers were spread around the room. They watched tensely, mouths set, eyes hard, as Jackson came on. *No*, he thought gloomily, *Doyle won't pull any aces out of this deck. If he threw down on Cameron, ten men would blast him out of his boots.*

Jackson stopped at Cameron's table just as Nate Croft halted beside it. Croft moved back uneasily. The rancher saw that Cameron looked sick. Roth's treatment had done him no good.

"Where is he?" Jackson asked harshly.

"We lost him," Cameron said.

Jackson pivoted and found Nate Croft in his way, stubby and strong, his sleeves rolled back from hairy forearms. "Excuse me, Nate," he said. He pushed him aside and heard one of the glasses shatter. Croft murmured an oath. Jackson went behind the bar. Three bartenders stared at him uncertainly.

"Get out of there," Jackson told them.

They came out and he sauntered behind the bar, looking under it, kicking at crates and wadded rags.

"When do you swamp out the roaches, Nate?" he asked. "Election years?" He made an arm signal to Tom Doyle. Doyle took a stack of yellow chips from a game table as he came. He flipped a chip into a cuspidor with a ring and a splash.

"Watch things," Jackson told him. "I'm going upstairs. Nate, you come, too," he decided suddenly.

His brother-in-law hesitated, glanced at Cameron's table, but accompanied Jackson up the short spiral staircase to the second floor. Jackson had taken a bracket lamp from behind the bar. He inspected the closets and a small storeroom. They walked down the rough-planked hall to Croft's bedroom over the street. Jackson drew his Colt.

"You first, Nate."

Nate's oily brown skin was sweating. He stared at the gun. He opened the door and stood there with the dark room before him. Jackson held the lamp high. "Inside," he ordered.

They went in. There was nothing but the smell of Croft's bedclothes, the disordered bachelor's gather, the tattered green blind. Jackson satisfied himself that Becket was not there. Croft watched him rigidly. Jackson holstered his gun and patted Croft's cheek.

"Nate, if I find him in this building ... if I find he's even been here ... what I do to you will make this town honest for forty years."

Red Roth entered from the back as he descended the stairs. Jackson drifted on and put his hands on the back of Troy Cameron's chair. Behind the colonel stood Tom Doyle. Doyle dropped a poker chip into the loose collar of the old man's shirt and chuckled as Colonel Edwards started.

"It's a small town, boys," Jackson said. "I'll have a man on every trail out of town. Make it easy on Becket and have him turn himself in."

"Shore will think about it," said Colonel Edwards. His eyes were sunken and dull. He looked tired enough to bury.

At the door, Jackson glanced back. Doyle was still staring at Cameron. "Ever fight a man from the front?" he asked him.

"Only on Sundays," Cameron said pleasantly.

"Sunday's comin'," Doyle said.

"Well, if I'm not at church," Cameron said. But although he was casually tilted back in his chair, he held his glass in his left hand and his right lay in his lap.

Doyle asked: "Why'd you quit marshaling? Rheumatism?"

Colonel Edwards twisted to glare at Jackson's gunman. "Why don't you get the hell out, Texas?"

Doyle leaned down to peer into the colonel's face. Then he

plucked the star from the old man's coat. "Hey! Bet you could help us, Colonel. You're marshal of this town, ain't you?"

"Paper-servin' marshal," Edwards said stiffly.

"Marshal just the same. Make me a deputy! Then I can really go after this killer."

"When I make you a deputy," Colonel Edwards sneered, "they'll make Geronimo a deacon in the church."

Doyle grinned and bent the star. He bent it back and it broke across the middle. "Mighty puny, at that." He dropped the pieces on the floor and swaggered after Jackson.

Dust, and a tightening cold, ruled the town. They stood before the saloon. Red Roth was cursing Doyle, low and bitterly.

"If you were an Indian," he told him, "they'd call you Chief Big Mouth. Thought you were going to give him a choice … standin' up or sittin' down. Well, he was sittin' down. But you were walkin' out."

Doyle's rough-featured face soured. "And only fifteen Defiance men backing him up. Go get him for me, Red. Tell him I'm waitin'. I'll take him on any time … but not all the nesters in Arizona."

"Tom's right," Jackson snapped. "If you want action, Red, it's here for the picking. Becket's in this town. We're going to flush him."

Squatting in the dirt, the big man made a map with his finger. "These here are livery barns. Go through 'em, Tom. Don't ask leave. Just make yourself at home." He cocked an eyebrow at Roth. "Red, use some of your orneriness in the Mexican joints. Dump over a few tables. Knock some greasers around. Let 'em know Big Jim is looking for somebody." His tawny eyes glinted as he rose. His face was like hardwood. "Tell them Jackson'll burn every Mexican saloon and store in town if I find a Mexican shielding him."

He stood there, tossing a fat .45 cartridge. "McCard," he told his range boss, "take the rest and go through some of the places where a man might hide, houses in close and any store that's open. Tell 'em who sent you."

A gusty relish for what was happening formed in him. Did

they think he couldn't keep up with changing times? There was a club called power that a man could always take in his two hands and swing with all his force, if he had the guts to—if he meant it and was not bluffing.

The men were mounting again. "Where will you be if we need you?" McCard asked. He was a tall man with the shape of a rifle and cool, intent eyes. He could take orders but act on his own.

"I'll be at the hotel. I saw my daughter's horse there. It's just possible," Jackson said, "that she may want to tell me something."

The hotel lobby was acrid with smoke of a mesquite-root fire snapping on a corner hearth. A door broke the rear wall, with a wicketed enclosure that was hotel desk and town post office combined at the right. Behind, a large, pudgy-featured man in a green eyeshade was reading a newspaper under a goosenecked student lamp. Ed Mattson rose hurriedly as Jackson came through the room. A few drummers in for the fall beef buying sat about the lobby.

"Howdy, Jim," he said with uncertain cordiality. Mattson's thin red hair was arranged with painstaking but ineffective art. "Which room is my daughter in?"

Mattson's eyes shifted to the key rack. "Serena?"

"I only had one daughter, at the last tally."

Mattson patted his scalp nervously. "Of course it's your business, Jim," he hedged, "but if I was you, I'd let her rest. She may be asleep already. She and the Becket girl come in pretty beat."

Jackson picked up the corroded pen lying on the register. "I'm going to shove this right through your windpipe if you don't answer me, Ed."

"Eleven," Mattson said hastily.

Jackson drifted down the hall and thumped on the door. When he spoke, Serena unlocked it. He went inside. He kicked the door shut with his spurred heel and glowered at her. She crossed her arms and turned away.

"Where's Becket?" Jackson said.

"I don't know. How would I?"

"How did you know he and Cameron weren't really going to trade hats and horses?"

"They must have changed back. When they passed me …"

Jackson's hand whipped her around. "Where is the harebrained little parcel of meanness?" he demanded.

"I can't tell you," she said.

"You can let Red Roth back out because I don't give him protection," Jackson said. "You can let Woodbury's bank foreclose me. But you can't tell me where Becket is."

"He'd be lynched, Dad. You know it."

"I told them I'd see him jailed and tried," Jackson told her.

She turned away again. "I can't tell you. I can't."

Jackson caught her wrist and yanked her back. He shoved her rudely against the armoire. "Wake up, ma'am! We aren't talking about next year's election. We're talking about being cleaned out. About us not having a three-cent nickel. We're talking about Miss Serena Jackson marrying a bullwhacker to keep herself in clothes and food, and Big Jim Jackson muscling hay bales in Will Mundy's feed barn."

Serena said huskily: "Gil Becket's sister is in the next room. She can hear us."

"I don't give a damn if the governor hears us!" Jackson shouted. "Somebody in this town is harboring a criminal. That somebody is going to wish to hell he hadn't, unless Becket's turned over."

"Dad," Serena said quickly, "there's something you don't know. Mike Saddler burned his friends' cabins and his own. Frances Becket and I found where he'd hidden all the things he didn't want to lose when he burned his own cabin. He had to burn it so that it would look like you'd done it. Then he engineered the raid on Roth's wagons. Don't you see it?" she pleaded. "After you whipped him yesterday, he had to be sure you and Troy's friends fought … or he'd have been the only one we foreclosed."

Jackson received it slowly.

"Don't you understand, Dad, why you must go easy now?" Serena continued. "Talk to Troy. Talk to Roth. It can be worked out. I know it can."

"And I know Red Roth," Jackson said with gloomy decision. "He's tough. He's simple. He's the kind of man who'll tattoo Mother on his chest, march in Fourth of July parades, and strip the living hide off a man who does a friend of his a bad turn. But he's mean as a rattlesnake when he's crossed. Do you think he'll go along with me before somebody's paid for the murder of Deke Howard?"

Serena shook her head. "But he'd never consider jailing sufficient punishment, because the hanging might not be for weeks … if ever."

Jackson hesitated a moment. "Serena, what he does with Becket is no affair of ours. Becket asked for it when he shot that logger. If I have to give him Becket to survive, he gets him."

"And that's why I won't tell you where he is."

Jackson clenched his fists, then let them relax. Well, no rush. She wanted to sound tough. Her own woman. But when he applied the pressure, she'd come through. He opened the door.

"Be thinking about marrying that bullwhacker," he advised. "If Roth leaves, we've got just sixty days before they close us out."

XV

After Jackson's crowd left the Pima Bar, there was some lackluster poker and drinking among the Defiance men. These men were exhausted and worried; Troy himself could scarcely move without groaning. Colonel Edwards fell asleep at the table, his head pillowed on his arms. Mike Saddler dealt cards to Troy and Bob Briscoe, and then he growled: "Pick 'em up, boys."

Troy pushed his cards away. "If I've got any luck left, I don't want to waste it on poker."

Saddler shrugged. He was the freshest and least concerned of all. With its adobe walls and oiled-earth floor, the saloon was cold and cheerless as a mine. Troy shook the colonel gently. "How about some food, old-timer?"

Colonel Ike rubbed his face with his hands, affected a miraculous recovery, and got up, staggering a little. "Bill and Emma ought to be open. Come on."

They went into the street. Eight Defiance Mountains men left the saloon and a few, grown serious about their liquor, stayed

behind. They were at the corner when a girl called Troy's name. She
stood across the street. He could not see her but he knew her voice.

"That's Becket's sister," he told the others. "I'd better talk to her."

"Big sacrifice?" Saddler asked with a wink at Briscoe.

"Not too big," Troy conceded.

The men walked down the side street to where a couple of
wagons were parked before a café. Crossing the street, Troy saw the
girl come from the alcoved doorway of an apothecary shop. She
wore a shawl over her head, pulled closely about her face. As Troy
reached her, she gave him her hand.

"Thank you," she said. "For saving his life, Troy, even if you
couldn't keep him out of trouble."

He did not know how to reassure her. He said: "We'll get it all
straightened out once we get him to Tucson."

"Of course." She smiled. Framed by the shawl, her features were
simple and sweet and beautiful. He kept on holding her hands, and
he had a strong urge to draw her to him. As if she sensed it, she drew
them away. She shivered.

"I've been waiting until I'm cold through!"

"Why didn't you send Mattson for me?"

"I didn't want anyone to know we were together. I'm so afraid
they'll find out where Gil is. Reverend Stiles says everything is
fine. But how long can it stay fine, with Jackson trying to force
Serena to give Gil away?"

Men were moving down the boardwalk toward them. "How
does he know she helped Gil?" Troy asked quickly.

"Because she lied to him today to throw him off the trail. I
heard them in her room a little while ago. He was trying to make
her tell him where Gil is hiding. I was afraid she might give in."

"Not Serena." Troy smiled. "You know, in her way, she's as tough
as her father. She'll hold out until we get Gil to Tucson."

"Just the same," she said, "I wish he could be moved tonight,
while it's dark."

He heard the men on the boardwalk stop a few stores away, rattle a locked door, and move on. "Not with Jackson's men on the prowl," he said.

She did not argue it. In the raking wind, they stood in the alcove. Along the street, the lamps shone with a frosty nimbus of dust. "There's something else," Fran said at last. "We found something strange at Mike Saddler's cabin. Serena thought it meant a lot. Most of his valuables were stored in the spring house. Serena seemed to think it meant he'd burned his own cabin."

She went on to explain Serena's theory of why Saddler would have done it. Troy felt suddenly tired and depleted. Saddler and his hellish sweat to be making trouble. Turning them against Jackson, and Jackson against them. Striking sparks for their tinder. Saddler, out on a limb unless there was a war.

"Fran, I'll take you back to the hotel," Troy said shortly. "Saddler's down at the café. I'm going to put it to him."

Spurred boots came on to the store next to where they stood, stopped, and some men rattled the door. The voice of Owen McCard said something. The men strolled on to the apothecary shop. Fran glanced quizzically at Troy. He squeezed her hand and turned to face the street. Two men started to head into the alcoved entrance. Then one saw them and put out his arm to halt the other, staring at Troy and Fran. His hand dropped to his Colt. It was Owen McCard, Jackson's lean range boss.

"Leave it alone, McCard," Troy said.

McCard's shoulders slackened. "Cameron!" he exclaimed. "What ...?"

"Don't you bird dogs have a home?" Troy asked.

McCard squinted at Fran. "Ain't that Becket's sister?"

"Yes. I think you ought to take off your hats."

He said it very seriously, and McCard and the other man reached up automatically to tip their hats.

Frances Becket said soberly: "How do you do? Are we in your way?"

McCard glanced at Cameron, found no comfort there, and looked at his companion. "No, ma'am. Just thought the store might be open. Well, Abe, I reckon we'd better ..."

"You're a good influence on McCard," Troy said as the pair left. "I never saw him smile before."

She looked up, her eyes too innocent. "I'm afraid I'm not doing your reputation any good, Troy. First I arrive in a flurry of red and take you off to the mountains. Now I'm seen in a dark doorway with you. Your young lady won't like it a bit."

Something told Troy that she had become quite conscious of him for himself, not merely as a friend of Gil's. At the same time he was acutely aware that she was very young, extremely attractive, and that her lips were moist and beautifully shaped.

"My young lady," he agreed, "probably wouldn't like it, except that she understands the situation."

He kept looking into her face, while the excitement in him strengthened. He was going to kiss her. He knew that. But under the circumstances, he didn't know what excuse to make. Still he was going to do it and worry about complications afterward. He saw her smile fade. She acted abashed but excited, also.

"Well...," she said weakly, "well, I suppose ..."

His hands opened her cape and found her body warm and soft. He pulled her against him. Her cape fluttered in the wind, but inside they were warm, pressed together. Her face turned up and they kissed eagerly.

She was pushing him away. He let her go. Her eyes were all pupils; her face was pale. He felt she must understand what had happened, but did she? It had happened to both of them, but had she seen it exactly as he did? Because the strange thing was that his making love to her did not seem to alter his feeling for Serena.

His Stetson had fallen. He turned to find it. When he rose, he said nervously: "Now we've got something to forget together. I'm quite sure my young lady wouldn't understand that."

They started for the hotel. The hard cut of the wind began to cool him.

"No, I don't think any girl would," Fran said. "No girl would like to think that it could be that way with any other girl."

He took her arm, watching the tips of her boots as they moved in and out under her cape. He felt she should understand, so he spoke very carefully.

"It's funny how you can love one person," he said, "and like another very much, and yet ..."

She smiled faintly. "Now, which person am I, I wonder?"

"Fran, don't misunderstand me ..."

She put her hand on his arm. "Troy, I do understand. I'm grateful for your help. Only I hope you'll be sure to understand yourself."

She went into the hotel. Disturbed, he pushed his hands into the pockets of his jacket and crossed the street. That had been a stupid thing to do. She would make much of it, and he would feel like a philanderer.

Remembering Saddler now, he walked down the street that tilted from the center toward some small homes and leafless orchards. Reaching Bill and Emma's Café, he halted and tried to see in through the window, but it was steamed over. He went in. The men were all at the counter drinking coffee while the cook filled their orders. His name was Bill Aperance and he went in for stake races and mustaches. This year he was wearing an imperial, his short black whiskers silver streaked, like the withers of a silvertip grizzly. He called to Troy.

"Tell Saddler that bay of Mundy's could beat his Morgan wearing cast-iron shoes!"

Saddler was at the near end of the counter. Troy took the stool beside him. Aperance thumped a gilded mustache cup before him. "If I told him that," Troy said, "I'd be in a bet in thirty seconds, and everybody'd lose but you."

He noticed Saddler watching his reflection in the glass door of the china cupboard behind the counter. The counterman started to pour his coffee, stopped suddenly, and said: "*Whoops!* That's the house cup." He always kept the last, bitter cup for himself. "What's new with Becket's sister?" he asked.

Saddler's reflected features sharpened. Troy warmed his hands on the cup. "Worried," he said.

"What happened up there, boys?" Aperance asked in a low, confidential tone.

There was an embarrassed hush. "Don't know for sure yet," Troy said. "Mike," he asked, "what was it you told us you saved from the fire?"

Saddler's thick hand, lying on the counter near Troy's, began to close. "I didn't make an inventory, if that's what you mean. I did get a few things out."

"A table and a butter mold, you said. Anything else?"

Saddler stiffly turned his stool to stare at him. "A few things, I said. I put them in the spring house for shelter."

Troy saw him touch his lips with his tongue; nervousness dried a man's mouth. "Things like furniture. A clock. Bullet molds. Pans. All your clothes. Things like that, Mike?"

Saddler stood up and stepped away from the counter. "What's on your mind?"

Troy swung his stool. "After we left, the women found everything but the kitchen stove in your spring house. I thought you said you barely saved yourself."

"Most of that stuff was already stored there. I didn't want Joe and Bill fouling it up."

Troy saw the dark face of Joe Wiley watching him. But Bill Thorne, Saddler's other man, faced rigidly away.

"That's right," Wiley said. "We might as well 'a' been sleeping in a tree."

No one smiled.

"That's queer, Mike," Troy pursued, "because when I was past your place a couple of weeks ago, it looked pretty well furnished. When did you decide Joe and Bill couldn't be trusted?"

Along the counter other men were twisting to stare at Saddler. Colonel Edwards stood up, his thin features whetting. Saddler held his big, ruddy face steady, but Troy saw his desperation.

"Look, if there's something you're tryin' to say …"

"There is, Mike. I say you burned your own cabin. But first you moved out everything you could store."

The wind could be heard trying the edges of the door. Bill Aperance laughed nervously. "That's a hell of a thing to accuse a man of, Troy."

Color flooded Saddler's face. "Do I act crazy enough to …" His voice choked in his throat.

"You'd have to be crazy not to burn your own cabin, after burning ours," Troy pointed out. "Yesterday you had a fight with Jackson. You tried to sell us out and even Jackson couldn't stomach that. He told you he was going to foreclose you first and you decided you'd better be sure of some friends. So you burned us out, and then talked us into raiding Roth's wagons to be sure Jackson was ready to fight, too."

Colonel Ike moved in on Saddler. The old face of the pioneer rancher twisted. "They don't come rottener," he said. "A buzzard would lose color at the smell of you."

Saddler hit him.

The old man lurched back against the counter. He sat down, his scuffed yellow boots thrown outward. Saddler regained his balance quickly as Troy came at him. Troy swung hard at his jaw and Saddler tilted a shoulder to take the ripping force of the blow. He staggered back, recovered, and slashed at Troy's jaw. Troy blocked it and threw a roundhouse punch that hit Saddler on the ear. Saddler fell against a table. A table leg crumpled under his weight and a lazy Susan of condiments shattered on the floor as he fell with the table.

He rolled over on his face, rested a moment, and got up. Now he came cautiously toward Troy, pressing his lips together, his breath snorting through his nostrils.

Something whistled over their heads and crashed against the adobe wall. Plaster and broken glass littered the floor. Aperance, the proprietor, stood there with a second water tumbler in his hand.

"Lookee, boys," he said dryly, "I'm running a chophouse, not a boxing club."

Colonel Edwards was getting up shakily, his thin white hair mussed. Bob Briscoe held one of his arms. Saddler moved across the room to help, but the old man bared his teeth like a wolf.

"Bunch quitter!" he snarled.

Saddler walked to where his coat hung from a deer horn. He laid it over his arm. Joe Wiley and Bill Thorne joined him. Saddler gazed stiffly at Troy.

"I'm no bunch quitter, Cameron. Someday you'll know that. It's up to you whether you believe me or Big Jim Jackson's girl."

"I hate to think," Troy said, "that I could figure a man so wrong."

He sat down before his coffee again and turned his back on Saddler. One by one, the others turned from Saddler. Aperance went to the big wood stove in the rear.

"How's that steak of mine doing?" the colonel asked.

Aperance threw the steak on a plate and brought it forward. "Hope you like 'em well done," he said uneasily.

The colonel looked at the steak, and then at Troy. "That there's a Mike Saddler special," he said. "Burned to cinders."

Troy heard the door close behind Saddler. He thought of Gil Becket in the drafty belfry of the church.

XVI

As the wind died, the cold tightened its fist on the town. Saddler stood on the corner with the Basque and Bill Thorne. He remembered his friends' faces as he left—like faces looking at him from an old tintype. Like those of people he had known long ago and left behind. He heard Wiley pop a match with his thumbnail and smelled the sulfur as he lighted a cigarette with his Stetson for shelter. Wiley blew out the smoke.

"Gonna take out part of your pay in calves, Bill?" he asked. "The boss man said we could."

"Shut up," Saddler snapped. "The deal with the bank is still on."

"With everybody in town down on you?" Wiley archly contained his anger.

"That's now. But that's where I'm different from a lot of people. I ain't quitting. There's other ways …"

"Will they work after they jug us for setting fires?"

"Any law against storing furniture in a spring house?" Saddler retorted. His head ached from Cameron's fist. He was trying to put something together. This town was a stick of blasting powder, and there had to be a match for it somewhere ... He gazed at the dark bank building. Woodbury held some notes of Jackson's, but they weren't due yet. Nate Croft then. Croft hated Jackson because Jackson had helped him once and made a second-rate relation out of him. He'd heard Croft had tried to buy into Anvil since Jackson had been in money trouble. Red Roth was dying to get his hands on Gil. Gil! Maybe he was the key. Saddler's blood hastened a little. *Hell, no,* he thought disgustedly. *They'll find the little fool, but I won't sell him out. Bet I could find him, though.*

Wiley turned up the collar of his coat and studied the black sky. "Hear they've had some good rains up on the Verde," he said. "Ought to be work up there, Bill. Seems like when it rains, there's plenty of work and ranchers don't mind paying for it. I mean with money, not promises."

Saddler drew a money poke from his pocket. "I'll pay you both off right now, if that's how you want it. But if you'll gamble another twenty-four hours of your time, the deal we talked about may still be good."

His thin face sardonic, Joe Wiley said: "Can you give us a rough idea how you're going to pass this miracle?"

"I'm going to borrow money to pay off the note on my place. That'll clear me. Then ..."

"Who's going to loan you the money?"

"Bank, maybe. Will you leave that to me? Otherwise, you can get the devil out and you won't be missed. But either way, shut your mouth or get out."

Wiley smiled. "All right. I'll shut up so you can think. See you around tomorrow."

He and Thorne walked toward the plaza, dark hulks heading up the road.

Mike Saddler walked stiffly to the Pima Bar. Tomorrow everyone in town would know about him and it would mean a fight every time he went in the saloon. The place was crowded, but he found a hole at the bar and ordered whiskey. Behind the bar, Nate Croft drifted to his place. Croft's whiskers had come through the greasy skin; his jaws looked like the backside of a slab of bacon.

"How's the cattle king?" Croft asked him.

"What's that mean?" Saddler took the sting of the whiskey into his mouth.

"Hear you're figuring to run Anvil for the bank after Jackson loses it."

"Who told you that?"

"Jim Jackson," Croft said. "Way he tells it, though, he's takin' over your A-Bar after you lose it."

Saddler appraised the saloonkeeper contemptuously. *He spends his money like an Indian*, he thought. *Gold in his teeth, embroidered vest, a watch seal it would take two men to lift. God, to have money like that!* "Why don't you loan me the money to pay him off?" Saddler grinned suddenly. "Be worth it to hear him yell, wouldn't it?"

"Dang' near."

"Pay 'em all off," Saddler joked. "Then he'd be under the forked stick again. No notes, no foreclosures."

"Yeah, I guess." Nate shrugged.

All at once Saddler tensed. He stared at the saloonkeeper. Something tremendous commenced growing in him. He began to grin. He suppressed it at once and glanced at the men on either side of him. One was playing poker dice with a companion. The other man, half drunk, was moodily frowning into his drink.

"Nate, I got to talk to you," Saddler said in a low voice.

"If this is about money," Croft hedged, "I ..."

"This is about more money than either of us ever had his fingers on," Saddler breathed. "Upstairs, Nate. Come on."

Croft's room above the saloon smelled like a bunkhouse, the air soaked with liniment, musty blankets, and dust. While Croft lighted a lamp, Saddler took a short-barreled rifle from a rack above the bed. He stood facing the window, as wide as the frame of it, black-haired, rugged.

Seeing him looking down on the village, Croft said: "Wonder where Becket's at, eh?"

"Lots of roofs down there, Nate. Lots of windows. Bet a smart man could flush him, though."

"You a smart man?" Croft joshed.

"Smart enough to whip Jim Jackson," Saddler said, turning. He couldn't stop grinning. He had control now—had the wild horse locked between his spurs and the bit. He moved about, rubbing the carbine. The bigness of it burned in him. "Nate, with your help I can snub him down tonight. How'd you like to go pardners with me on Anvil?"

Croft's black eyes pinched. "How many whiskies did you have before I came along?"

"If I'm drunk, a man was never sober. You got a few thousand dollars cash?"

Croft examined him coldly. "That's no damned business of anybody's."

"If you did have, Nate, you'd be rich in a year or two. Because we could buy in with Jackson, run the show ourselves, and make something out of that ranch."

"Anvil ain't for sale."

"Anything's for sale, Nate, if a man's in bad trouble. Suppose you were to loan all us Defiance men the money to pay Jackson off on those notes? He couldn't touch our timber then. He'd starve out in three months."

"That don't put us on Anvil."

"No. But if we gave Jackson a choice between selling us a piece of Anvil, and freezing him out by backing those ranchers, he'd sell. What else? He's beat for sure if the notes are paid. But if he gives us sixty percent of Anvil, he's going to think … I'm still floatin'. Maybe I can outfox them yet."

Croft grunted: "*Hmm.*" He slipped his thumbs into the armholes of his flowered vest. "Where's the joker?"

"No joker, Nate. Clear my place ... six hundred dollars ... give me ten percent of Anvil, and we'll put that ranch in the black in a year. We'll foreclose all those mountain ranches. Then we'll skin the timber out. Woodbury's bank won't have room enough for all the money we're going to make." He dropped the rifle on Croft's cot and took him by both shoulders. "Don't you see it, Nate? We'll buy up other ranches. We'll freeze Jackson out in a couple of years. You'll be wearing gold caps on every tooth and diamonds as big as buggy lamps."

Croft began to catch fire. But he hung back. "I'm no rancher, Saddler. I went broke once ranching."

"You won't have to set foot on Anvil if you don't feel like it. I got ideas enough for both of us."

"Well, I'd have to ..."

Saddler pulled him back. "That's it, Nate. There ain't time to dicker. Once he starts cuttin' trees, we'll never get him out of those mountains. We've got to slap him with it tonight."

Croft gazed at him with a faint, resentful grin. "Not bad for you, my friend. I buy into Anvil and you get ten percent and your own place cleared. Just for the idea."

"Oh, no," Saddler said. "For the guts to brace Jackson and Cameron's crowd. Just step up and tell Jackson you're taking over Anvil if you think you can swing it yourself. I'll help you collect your teeth."

Croft lifted a deprecating shoulder. "If I didn't think you were worth ten percent, Mike, I wouldn't even talk about it. I was joking."

"Good," Saddler said. "Because I might walk out right in the middle of things just to prove it." Then he peered into Croft's polished little eyes. "OK, Nate?"

Croft moistened his lips. "Well ..."

With the heel of his hand, Saddler buffed his shoulder. "Good! Send somebody for Jackson."

* * * * *

For a while he was alone in the room. He turned down the lamp and stood at the window. All the south end of town lay beneath him—Front Street, the plaza, the random blocks of small adobe buildings. He could see some men on the walk, and two riders jogged past with their collars turned up and rifles under their arms.

All those years of string saving, Saddler swept them from his mind like trash. Now the ideas, the ability, the energy he had stored so long would be spent rapidly.

Something was going on in the row of Mexican stores at the east end of the plaza. A man was holding a hurricane lamp. A fight seemed to be in progress before a cantina. After a while some men went inside. Then he saw two men walk from the gap in the wall and come down Front Street. By his bulk, he knew one of them was Jim Jackson. He saw a man approach him on the walk—one of Croft's barkeepers. Then Jackson stared up at the window where Saddler stood.

He heard Croft coming back. Saddler turned up the lamp as Croft slipped inside. "He's comin', Mike. Are you sure …?"

"Cigar, Nate." Saddler put out his hand and Croft put a cigar in it. Saddler lit it over the lamp. He picked up Croft's rifle and opened the breech. It was loaded. Croft made a nervous sound in his throat.

Big Jim Jackson's heavy boots made the stairs creak. Saddler set the gun against the wall at the end of the cot. He sat on the cot and cocked one leg across his knee. The knob turned and a man banged the door open. Jim Jackson, frowning, moved into the entrance. His big, square face with its cavalryman's mustache was harsh and a small cut showed over his eye. So Saddler knew he had been involved in the ruckus in the plaza.

Saddler said: "Spend a lot of your time scrappin' these days, Jackson. Beatin' up greasers, now?"

"I had an idea Ramon Corral knew something about Becket. Maybe you'd be interested in what I told him. Anybody we find shielding Becket will get the same thing Becket gets."

Saddler puffed on the cigar. "Come on in."

Contempt burned in Jackson's eyes. "Don't reckon I could stomach the two of you in the same room. What've you got to sell this time?" He stopped and blinked. "Wait a minute!" he said abruptly. "You sellin' Becket?"

Saddler shook his head. "No. We're buying something. A share of Anvil."

He saw Jackson fill his lungs, took note of the square shoulders filling the corduroy coat, the thick brown pillar of his neck. "This," Jackson said, glancing suspiciously at Nate, "smells like something hatched in a saloon. I don't know who thought this would be funny, but I'm going to lick him with one hand."

Saddler rose. "Nate's thinking of buying up all those Defiance Mountains notes. If he does, that'll leave you on the short end of the rope. Because you won't have any timber to sell, or money to pay the bank."

Saddler saw him falter, saw him going sick inside, like a snakebit man settling down to watch his leg blacken.

"But like I told Nate," he went on, "there's a better way to do this. Save Jackson's hide and save mine. Instead of putting that money into the notes, let's give it to Jackson ... for sixty percent of Anvil."

Downstairs, a piano tinkled. Jackson started across the room, his face thunderous. Saddler put his cigar in his mouth and picked up the rifle. Jackson stopped, his hands hanging.

"Don't even look like you were coming at me again," Saddler said. "Big Jim! Nothing big about you but the size of your blunders. You thought you had me cornered, didn't you? But now I'm talking and you're listening."

Jackson said nothing. A corroding hatred brimmed in his eyes.

"We're leaving you forty percent. That means I'll be making sixty percent of the noise around Anvil. I'm going to show you how to make money with that ranch, Jackson."

Jackson said sardonically: "You can't make money without range. Even a boy wonder like you."

"We'll have the range. We're foreclosing those notes and taking over the Defiances. We'll cut timber, and a lot of those starved-out pastures like Becket's are going to grow some grass at last. But you're going to set still and listen. You can do all your talking in the saloons ... if anybody will listen to you."

The corners of Jackson's mouth began to quirk. Uneasiness touched Saddler. "Well?" he said.

"Can I talk for a minute?" Jackson asked. "You see, I don't own those notes. So I can't sell them."

"Don't give me that, when you've just been threatening fore-closure. Stiles sold you the notes with the store."

"But I put the notes in Serena's name, so she'd have something left if I went under."

He began to laugh. Saddler glanced at Croft. Croft looked absolutely stricken.

"Then get them back from her," Saddler said. "You'd have had to do that to foreclose us."

"I tried," the rancher said. "She wouldn't sell. So I figured to move you out first and foreclose after."

"She'll turn them over if she knows you're licked," Saddler insisted.

Jackson shrugged. "Maybe. Talk to her. Maybe you can make her believe she's not geared for poverty. I couldn't."

Saddler juggled the carbine in his hands.

"And when you get that fence jumped," Jackson continued, "jump another. How are we going to keep Red Roth if he don't get Becket?"

Saddler scratched his neck. "I don't know. Maybe I could find Gil. We could get him to jail before Roth strung him up, maybe. But we won't get any place with Cameron in the way."

Jackson measured him speculatively. For the first time he really seemed interested. "If you can deliver Becket, I can handle Cameron."

"How?"

"Let me worry about that. It comes to this. Get the notes from Serena, give me Gil Becket, and we're in business."

"Sixty-forty," his brother-in-law said.

"Sixty-forty."

Croft found paper and pen and made three copies of a brief document. They signed the papers, each took his own copy, and Saddler, with exhilaration burning in him, abruptly offered his hand, grinning. He pulled it back the instant he saw the expression in Jackson's eyes.

"If friendship's in the contract, too," Jackson drawled, "I'm backing out right now."

When the rancher reached the door, Saddler said quickly: "What about Cameron?"

"Do you know where he is?" Jackson asked.

"Him and the rest went over to Bill and Em's a while ago."

"Find him," Jackson told Nate. "Tell him I want a powwow."

"Here?"

"Hell, no." Jackson settled his hat. "In the plaza. At the corner of the church. Don't bother Serena tonight," he added to Saddler. "After tonight she'll be easier handled."

XVII

Troy was pulling on his coat when Croft came in. They had eaten, some of the men had drifted back to the saloon, and now the colonel was telling about wild horse trapping in the Big Bend country. " … Slapped my iron on forty-six mustangs in three weeks! Just me and a couple of Mexicans."

Troy had been thinking about Gil Becket. Terriers like Gil should not try to run with timber wolves like Saddler. They got hurt every time. The wolf killed the calves and the terrier got shot for it.

He thought about Gil's sister. Considering everything, she was holding together very well. He remembered the thrill of kissing her.

At that moment Croft came in, chafing his hands together. Croft was wearing a high black derby that gave him stature, and a black short coat with a velvet collar. Croft's eyes darted nervously at Troy. Troy nodded to him and went out. In a moment Croft followed him.

"Say, Troy, I've got a message for you," Croft said. "Jim came in a few minutes ago. He wants to see you."

"If it's about Becket, he's not for sale," Troy said curtly.

"I don't think it is. I trust Jim just about as far as I can see him, it's true. But he's worried, and I reckon he's playing it straight this time."

"What's he want to see me about?"

"He didn't say ... not exactly. He took a couple of drinks with me and began to open up. He said ... 'Nate, this town's going to blow up if I don't do something about it pretty soon. Where's Cameron?' he asked me. I said I'd get you. It sounds like he's ready to make you an offer."

Troy considered as they walked on. "Maybe he's coming to the snubbing post at that. You know, I never saw him as ornery as he's been acting lately."

"Well, I won't argue with you," Croft grunted. "But I said I'd get you. He said he couldn't talk to you where he'd be seen, though. Roth might draw some wrong conclusions. He said he'd talk to you in the plaza. Over near the church."

Troy eyed him narrowly. Something in Croft's tone aroused his suspicions. Still, Croft and his brother-in-law were hardly to be thought of as conspirators. "When?" he asked.

"He's waiting now."

They reached the Pima Bar. Croft shivered inside his short coat. "Cold," he murmured. "Got to get those winter doors up." He went inside.

He's in a hell of a hurry, Troy thought.

He crossed Front Street, but then, instead of turning down to the main gate of the old town hall, he took the side street that followed the west wall of the plaza. About half a block down there was a small gate through which Mexican goatherds brought their milch goats every morning. Troy stood here and scanned the plaza—the line of Mexican shops against the far wall, the corrals for bull teams in the middle, and off to the right, the belfry of Stiles' little church rising, low and thick, against the sky. A softly plucked guitar sang in a cantina. Troy settled his hat, but could not lose the feeling he had. Near the church, under a gaunt desert cedar, a horse was rubbing against the bark. Troy started across the plaza.

The pony looked around as he came near. It was not one of Jackson's big horses. It was a smaller animal, and the night sparkled on bits of silver in its bridle. He walked very slowly toward the church. He was coming at it from the west now instead of the north—as anyone waiting here would have expected. He could not see the man waiting around the corner. He skirted the steps of the church. He put his hand on his Colt. But if it were actually Jim Jackson, he could not go in with a gun in his hand. He let the gun remain in its holster.

As he moved on, he kept his eyes on the eroded adobe corner of a building. He did not see the stone until his boot came down on it and he stumbled. At once he caught his balance. But a man had stepped from behind the church, his hand on his gun.

"Who is it?" Tom Doyle's voice snapped.

In the shadows, he had not made Troy out yet. Troy eased his gun from the holster. "It's me, Doyle. Did we have a date?"

Doyle's body turned sidewise. He had the reflexes of an animal. He was as fast as Troy had heard. Troy aimed at his thigh and fired. The gun flash showed Doyle with an unlighted cigarette in his lips, his gun lining out, his Stetson on the side of his head. The roar was tremendous. Troy's hand kicked high with the recoil as he stepped away.

Doyle's gun went off and instantly Troy was blind and deaf. He stood there very still, his gun cocked. He heard Doyle go down, heard him swear sobbingly, and cock his gun again. Over the strings of that Mexican guitar a hand had fallen. Voices called from the cantinas, and in the street beyond the plaza men shouted and a horse ran hard.

Then he could see Doyle dimly. The gunman had dropped his Colt and was sitting on the ground, rocking back and forth and holding his leg.

Troy stepped in and kicked the gun away. He remembered Gil. He hoped Gil would keep his mouth shut and not give himself away.

"Who sent you?" he asked Doyle.

Doyle's savage eyes turned up. "Nobody ... sent me," he groaned.

"Jackson sent Croft to toll me over here. Where is he now?"

"No damned business creeping up on a man," Doyle panted. "I was ... waiting for Jackson."

"Did you have a date with him, too?"

Doyle slumped over, moaning deep in his throat. He did not answer. Troy took his gun from the ground. "I'll send a doctor," he said, "and have them fix up a bed for you at the hotel. There'll be a lock on the door, and you'll stay there until you can be moved to the jail."

He heard them coming across the plaza. Probably Roth and Owen McCard and the rest. He strode to Doyle's horse, untied it, and toed the stirrup. It bolted as he swung up. He swerved it toward the west wall and left the plaza. He felt half sick, churning with the excitement and fear that hit a man after such action.

Then he remembered Jim Jackson.

Unless this deal had been between Nate Croft and Doyle— Croft's favor to a valued customer—Jackson had turned a bend in his trail. Murder was one of the cards he held now. A man like that could only be stopped one way. Troy had tried to avoid anything like that; he had preached to his friends a go-slow doctrine. And all he had done was to prove, once again, that direct action was often the safest and the fairest method, even though it might involve brutality.

* * * * *

In the morning it was as if a wind had scoured the country for days, and then had passed. The silence seemed unnatural. During the night Nate Croft had put up his winter doors with their leaded-glass panes, and had padlocked them. He did not unlock them now. The stores were open but there was no traffic. Troy and some other ranchers who had passed the night in Mundy's hay barn breakfasted at Bill and Emma's. No one had seen Mike Saddler. As Troy left the restaurant, Colonel Ike Edwards came down the walk from Front Street, his long black coat buttoned tightly. The colonel caught Troy's arm, his old hawk's face tense.

"Don't go up there, Troy," he said. "Jackson's bunch is in front of the hotel. McCard, Roth, and about a dozen others. Joe Wiley and Bill Thorne, too, by God."

"What are they doing?"

"Just blockin' traffic. But nobody better go up unless everybody goes up." He grunted. "What the hell are we going to do about Gil?"

"Get him out," Troy said shortly. "Hear anything about Doyle?"

"Doc Watkins was leaving when I went by. Bad news. He says he'll make it if the hole you put in him don't infect."

"How bad is he?"

The old rancher's eyes soured. "Meaning no discredit, Troy, but you shore bungled that job. You had five feet eight of Doyle to shoot at, and you put one hole down low on his thigh. You didn't even shatter the bone, Watkins says. He says Jackson's going to move him out to the ranch."

From where Troy stood, a little wedge of Front Street was visible. A man drove a buggy past, the horse trotting smartly. He could see no one on the walk. The trigger was set and people were standing back. A note of complaint entered the colonel's voice.

"How are we going to get him out with them perching here like buzzards in a tree?"

"We'll have to move them out first."

"That sounds like a good trick," Edwards scoffed. "Can I watch you do it?"

"Today," Troy promised. "What if we all took off for the mountains about noon? Roth would probably figure we'd gone back to finish up on his gang. He'd demand protection from Jackson and he'd get it. Jackson would have to take most of his bunch out to follow us. As soon as it was dark, Gil could leave."

"Might serve," Edwards said.

"Got to serve. About noon, why don't you start the boys for the mountains?"

"What about you?"

"I'll rustle some good horses and stick around town. Somebody's got to go with Gil."

Edwards considered, nodded, and then his eyes grew melancholy. "It ain't the town I used to know, Troy. There's more trash around than men."

"It seems that way sometimes. But the air will clear. Tell the boys to think it over. Meantime I've got a man to see."

As he moved on, the colonel called: "Who's that?"

"Jim Jackson," Troy said. "I had an appointment with him last night, but we didn't get together."

Reaching Front Street, he saw the group before the hotel. Except here, the street was bleakly empty. Red Roth sat on the hitch rack talking to Owen McCard, who leaned against the rail beside him, his back to Troy. A clot of men blocked the hotel door. On a bench against the broken-plastered wall, Saddler's men, Wiley and Thorne, were present but set apart like poor relations of Jackson's crew. Troy wondered at their being included at all.

Roth saw him and touched McCard's arm. The range boss looked around, lean and hard. Then he turned back to speak to a cowpuncher who strolled into the hotel. There was not much rashness left in Troy Cameron after his gunman's years. But he had daylight and witnesses in his favor, and the very recent encounter with Tom Doyle. He did not know how Doyle had told it, but a few would realize Troy simply carried a faster gun.

With his left hand in his pocket, right hand free, he started for the hotel. They had all turned to watch. He stopped near the hitch rack. Roth's eyes were bloodshot and ugly, and the jaws he had not shaved for three days were rough with rusty gray stubble. McCard's face was cool and cautious.

"Is Jackson inside?" Troy asked them.

Roth looked at McCard. "Is he?"

"Not as I know," McCard said blandly.

Troy walked past them. In the group before the door he saw Mike Saddler. Troy stared at him, astonished by the contradiction of Saddler's presence. He was conscious of every man's slow wheeling like a compass needle to watch him. No aisle opened through the group of tight-mouthed men blocking the door. Troy said, "Excuse me, boys," and waited an instant. When a way did not open, he pushed a cowboy aside and walked into the group. The man swore and turned on him. But he stayed where Troy had pushed him, and Saddler, who still blocked the entrance, moved aside with sober features.

The lobby was smoky with warmth. Two beef buyers sat in one corner with out-of-town newspapers before their faces. An Anvil cowpuncher came from the hall to the back rooms, saw Troy, and stopped short.

"Is he coming out?" Troy asked him.

"Yeah," the man said. He walked outside.

In a moment a door closed and a man could be heard moving toward the lobby. Jackson came through the doorway, hard eyed, big as a legend, neatly dressed in his dark corduroy coat and black-and-gray striped trousers tucked into black stovepipe boots. His Stetson rode the side of his head. *He would never lose that masculine, battering-ram vigor*, thought Troy. Men would always get out of his way. But there was an edge to him that was unfamiliar, a haggardness in his eyes. He crossed the small room to Troy and planted himself, stiff-mouthed and silent.

"We were going to have a talk last night," Troy reminded him.

"Yes," Jackson agreed. "But you saw fit to bushwhack my ramrod before I got there. I was going to look you up afterward, but Serena stopped me. If I'd found you, I'd have killed you."

He meant it. The violence was still in him, but it had compressed to a bitter, controlled force.

"Because of Doyle?" Troy asked him. "I could have killed him. He knows that."

"You had the drop on him. He was waiting for me when you jumped him."

Peering deep into the tawny eyes, Troy said: "Croft told me it was you I was to meet. But I found Doyle there instead … with a gun in his hand."

"No," Jackson said. "Doyle's gun was in his holster. Yours was in your hand. I wanted Doyle to hear what went on when we talked. I sent a man to find him, and he got there before I did. And you came Injuning along and jumped him. I'm moving Doyle to my ranch this morning. You can try to stop him if you want."

"Out of town," Troy said, "is a good place for Doyle. There aren't so many corners for him to coyote around." He eyed Jackson in slow speculation. At last he said: "Once I had a fight with Mike Saddler over you. I claimed, if we gave you time, we could work out a compromise. You see, I thought I was a pretty good judge of men. Was I that wrong about you?"

"You were if you thought you could chouse me around like a yearling calf," Jackson said. "I offered a compromise and you didn't take it."

"A compromise that included starvation."

Jackson glanced beyond him at the crowd of men on the

boardwalk. He settled his Stetson. "Maybe you've got time to kill. I haven't. The offer I made before is still good. But any deal we make now will start with your surrendering Gil Becket."

"It's no deal, then."

"Adios," Jackson said. He gave Troy a glance and a nod, tucked his hands in his pockets, and strolled from the lobby. There was something absolutely final about it. Jackson had taken a course involving murder and lynching. It was the course a desperate man set himself, not a confident one. But it was final.

XVIII

Last night they had left their horses at Francisco's Livery Stable, across the alley from the hotel. Troy decided to make sure of horses for himself and Gil. He walked down the hall to the rear. In one of the rooms he could hear men talking—Tom Doyle and another man. He passed Serena's room and wished he could talk to her, but she would want assurance that everything was going to work out fine, and how could he give her that?

As he stepped into the alley, he was touched by the old caution that had kept him alive in a dangerous trade. The cold lay heavily in the alley. He glanced each way before he crossed. Within the barn it seemed colder. Horses stood in the stalls, pulling down hay from slatted cribs. While he was looking at his own horse, Pete Smeaton, the stableman, came from a tack room. His real name was Stevenson Smeaton, but for some reason he liked the name of Pete.

"Leavin'?" he asked Troy. His eyes sharpened with interest. He was dying to ask about the shooting. Smeaton was a spare, sandy-haired man with long sideburns and a rapid manner of speech.

"Not yet." He supposed Smeaton was reliable. Defiance men gave Francisco's barn all their trade when they were in town. But this was a no-limit game. "Some of these horses need shoeing, Pete. Can you get to it this morning?"

"Which ones?"

He looked the horses over and told him which to shoe. "We'll need them by three o'clock."

A door banged across the alley. Ed Mattson, the hotelkeeper, put his head in the door. "Pete, get Miss Jackson's buggy ready!"

"Keeps a man busy." Pete sighed as Mattson vanished. He took a lead rope from a peg. Suddenly he grinned at Troy. "What about Doyle, Troy? How'd it go?"

Troy smiled. "Went fine." He walked with him to the black crossbar buggy that belonged to the Jacksons. He had decided this was a sign either from Serena or the fates. He was supposed to wait.

"Did he throw down on you?" Smeaton asked eagerly.

"Pete, a man hardly knows what happened, after it's over," Troy told him.

Pete backed the buggy horse into the traces. "Well, I guess what I mean—"

"You mean," Troy supplied, "am I faster than Tom Doyle? No. I was just readier."

In a few minutes a girl's voice called into the dusk of the barn: "Pete? I'm ready."

"I'll take it," Troy said to the liveryman.

Pete opened the alley doors and he drove out. Serena stood in the thin winter light with a dark cape over her shoulders. Seeing Troy, she gasped. Then she smiled in quick pleasure and let Smeaton help her into the buggy. Troy spread the blanket over her lap and tucked it about her legs. Staring straight ahead, he said: "Where to, ma'am?"

"To … oh, anywhere, Troy, so we're together."

He decided to put the time doubly to use. There was a rear door to the church that passed through the back wall of the plaza. His plan was to go after Gil through that door tonight. He wanted to be sure of the ground first, since it would be dark when he brought the horses around.

As he drove, he reached over to take her hand. It felt small and cold.

"Do you know where I'd really like to go?" the girl said. "Away. To California. To Albuquerque. But away from here."

"So would I," Troy admitted.

"Then why don't you?" she asked suddenly.

Troy shrugged. "Loyalty, I suppose."

"To a man who murdered someone in a raid you didn't approve of?"

"I was in on it, whether I approved or not. So I can't quit Gil now."

He rounded a corner and they rolled down an aisle of china-berry trees, their withered, dime-size leaves whirling into the air behind the buggy.

"Particularly," Serena said thoughtfully, "when he has such a pretty sister. Did you have a pleasant evening with her?"

"McCard"—Troy sighed.—"has a busy mouth."

"Owen told Father, and of course Father told me. But if it hadn't been Owen, it would have been someone else. You can't keep a secret like changing girls in a town this size."

Troy stopped the buggy. Taking her by the shoulders, he made her face him. "I change horses," he said. "I change my politics. But I don't believe in changing girls when I've got a good one."

Suddenly Serena pressed her face against his shoulder. "I'm losing you," she whispered. "I'm losing you to her, and I don't know why."

"Serena, her brother's in trouble. Isn't it natural we should have been talking about it?"

"Did she send for you? Or did you go to her?"

Troy sighed. "She was waiting for me across from the Pima. She was worried about Gil."

Serena's head raised. "Then she'd heard Dad trying to make me tell where he was hidden."

"She couldn't help hearing. Naturally she was worried."

And it was odd that this same fear had been with him since last night. He could not say why, but he was afraid that Jackson, the tension in Frontera—something would break Serena down and cause her to inform on Gil.

"I knew she was listening," she said haughtily. "I told Dad to lower his voice, but it's something he's never learned. Sometimes I'm proud that he hasn't. If he has something to say, he says it."

"One way or another," Troy said dryly.

"What do you mean? You mean Tom Doyle, don't you?" she accused. "You think he was there to kill you."

"Possible," he said.

He swung the horses down the road following the back wall of the plaza, where two ruts had been cut by a generation of ox carts and wagons. Along this road he would ride one horse and lead Gil's and an extra tonight.

Serena said: "Aren't you afraid someone will see you here and guess where Gil is?"

He found himself unwilling to trust her with their plans. She had saved Gil, yet now he was afraid to trust her.

"I'm not going to stop," he said. "I thought he might make a sign that he's all right."

They passed the door in the wall. Above, the belfry of the church mounted low and blocky as a watchtower. The boarded-up arches gave no indication that a man was hiding there. They passed, the buggy came to the far end of the wall, and Troy turned toward Front Street.

"You'll try to get him out soon?" Serena asked.

"As soon as your father calls off his bird dogs." When they reached the corner, he got out.

"Back streets," she sighed. "How long will we be meeting on them, Troy?"

"Not much longer," he promised.

She gazed at him with a faint smile. "McCard seemed to think you were kissing her."

"McCard will have to be straightened out sometime," Troy said brusquely.

She kept looking into his eyes. "But you did kiss her after he left. Do you know how I know? I heard her singing to herself when she came back to her room. For a woman who was worried about her brother, that was very odd behavior, wasn't it?"

Troy said hopelessly: "I don't know. Since it has something to do with women, I wouldn't even guess."

XIX

All morning Fran had stayed in her room. She was afraid to go to Gil, afraid not to. She had come fifteen hundred miles and seen him only for a few frightening hours. She had heard Serena Jackson talking with her father again this morning, and Jackson had been rough and cavalier with the girl. Troy thought she would hold out against him. Fran was certain she would not.

About noon she decided to look for Troy again. It embarrassed her to be following him about. She wished he would come looking for her. But since he hadn't, she would have to go to him, because Gil must be moved. Then she heard men in the hallway. She stood perfectly still while they came to her door and halted, talking low. But a door across the hall opened and Jackson's voice said gruffly: "Ready to travel, Tom?"

Doyle muttered something. "Come on, then," Jackson told him. Then he spoke to someone else. "That's her room yonder. You'd better produce, mister."

Jackson and Doyle left. The other man walked slowly to Serena's door and rapped. Fran heard the springs of Serena's cot stir as she got up. After a moment of silence Serena said, "Dad?" and the door squeaked open. Fran heard Serena gasp. "You had no right coming without permission. Will you please take your foot away from the door?"

With a twist of humor in his voice Mike Saddler said: "What is this … a ladies' dormitory? I've got permission, Miss Serena. Your daddy sent me."

"That's a lie," Serena said.

"No, ma'am. I'll come in, if you don't care."

Fran stood in the middle of her room, wondering what she should do. She heard a sharp scuffle and the closing of the door. "Now," Saddler was saying, "just settle down to listening to me. Do you own those Defiance Mountains notes?"

"Who told you I did?"

"Your father. Nate Croft and I bought in with him last night. Now we need the notes so we can go ahead with our plans."

Serena gave a small laugh. "That is the most preposterous lie I ever heard. My father wouldn't sell a square inch of Anvil to you. I thought you understood that the day he whipped you."

"Yes, ma'am." You could hear the grin in his voice. "But last night I whipped him. Talked Nate into either paying off all those notes you hold, so your father'd be blocked, or buying in with him and we'd all go ahead together. We let Jackson make his own pick. Here's the paper he signed."

There was a silence. When Serena spoke again her voice sounded weaker. "What if I refuse to sign the notes over to you?"

"Let's not talk about refusing. Let's talk about signing. Otherwise we'll be talking about bankruptcy and a lot of other things neither of us would want to happen."

"What other things?"

"Well, like lynching."

Fran slumped onto the cot, staring at the wall.

"Where does lynching come into it?"

"It's all sort of mixed up together." A match scratched and gave its tiny sputter. Saddler sounded complacent. "You see, even after you give us the notes, you'll still have to give us that murderer. Because Roth won't cut trees while Becket's running around loose. Bad example, you see. And we'll get him. No doubt about it."

"You were Gil's friend," Serena said huskily.

"I'm still his friend. If Roth takes him, he hangs from the ridgepole of a hay barn. If your daddy and I take him, he goes to jail. That puts a ring in Roth's nose, so's he has to fill the contract. And maybe Gil will get off with jail. So how about it?"

Fran's pulses bounded. Her throat was so dry she could scarcely breathe.

"Why should I believe you?" Serena asked. "If it were true, my father would have come to me himself."

"Said he came last night. He thought maybeso a stranger could do better."

"Tell him to come again," Serena Jackson stated.

"He's done left with Doyle and the boys. Cameron's outfit took off a bit ago, and Roth was afraid they'd be hitting his wagon camp. So they all left. The road's clear now for me to take Becket over to jail. I expect you know," he drawled, "that there's going to be a war if you don't work with us. Because your father's going ahead anyway, and naturally those settlers will fight. But if he nails 'em down legally, they can't. That's quite a responsibility on you, ain't it? What's that little old watch of yours say?" Saddler asked.

"Elev ... eleven forty-five," Serena faltered.

"I'll be back at twelve. That's fifteen minutes. Be ready to tell me where Becket's hiding. Otherwise you're going to see a man get his neck stretched, Miss Serena, and it'll be your own fault. And I just wouldn't give a lot for your daddy's chances of getting any older, either."

As soon as he had gone, Fran rushed into the hall and opened

Serena's door. Serena was sitting on the bed. She gazed at Fran, pale as a candle.

"What am I going to do?" she whispered.

"Isn't there a marshal?" Fran asked.

"Yes, but he's an old man. And probably out of town with the rest. I ... I wonder if Troy went with them ..."

Fran stared down at the dark-haired girl sitting on the white candlewick bedspread. "You aren't thinking, surely, of ... of giving Gil away?"

"No, but what he said was true. If Roth finds your brother ..."

"But unless you betray him, Roth won't find him!" Fran cried.

Serena's eyes were bitter. "And if he never comes to trial, my father and I are through on Anvil."

"Miss Jackson," Fran pleaded, "is a ranch more important than a man's life?"

"We're talking about my father's life, too, according to Saddler."

"He's only trying to frighten you." Suddenly Fran knew she must find Troy, if he were still in town. She told Serena hastily: "Lock your door. Don't let him in when he comes back. I'm going to find Troy."

The last expression in Serena's eyes suggested calculation. Perhaps she was less afraid of Mike Saddler than Fran had thought. Less afraid of Saddler than of losing Anvil.

She hurried from the hotel, but then she did not know where to look for him. Finally she recalled the little restaurant down the street where Troy and his friends ate when they were in town. She entered but it was almost empty. The languorous counterman was talking with a man in a town suit and derby.

"Mister Aperance," Fran said, "I'm looking for Troy Cameron."

Aperance smiled. "Little lady, I wish I could help. But they've all took off to the mountains."

"Oh, no!"

"Something wrong?" Aperance inquired.

What could she tell him? What could anyone do who was not willing to risk his life for Gil's? "No, thank you," she said.

The Pima Bar had not unlocked its doors yet. As she stood across the street, she could see a man looking out of an upstairs window. She hurried on to the plaza and glanced along the line of Mexican shops, searched hastily through the bullwhackers' camp, and then gazed fixedly at the church. She saw no one she knew, and tears filled her eyes. She was frightened and hurt—hurt that Troy should leave Gil unprotected.

It must have been fifteen minutes now since she had left. She hurried into the rear of the hotel. Not a sound in the hall. The oiled flooring ran darkly to the front. Fran tapped at Serena's door, but the girl did not answer. She looked in. Serena's cape was gone. The room was empty.

Fran rushed into her room and looked in the armoire for the rifle Troy had lent her in the mountains. It was there, stubby, bronze-framed, heavy. *God give me strength!* she thought.

She walked out the back, the carbine under her cape, and returned to the plaza. The rifle banged against her leg as she approached the church. One of the large double doors was open. A bell rope dangled from the belfry. Suddenly a man appeared from a door at the right, big and fleshy and with bristling brows.

Her grip on the rifle failed and it clattered on the floor. The man stared at it. "By any chance," he asked, "are you Gil Becket's sister?"

"Yes! Then you're Reverend Stiles. Is ... is Gil all right?"

"He's all right." Fred Stiles smiled. "Come in. I usually ask worshipers to leave their guns outside, but since this is a special occasion ..."

Under his weight the old ripsawed flooring groaned. He placed the rifle against the wall.

"Sis?" She heard the voice above their heads, and turned quickly to glance up.

"Gil, you must come down! You've got to get away."

"Nothing I'd rather do, Sis, but I've got to wait for Troy. Saw him drive past the back of the church this morning. Figure it was a sign."

"Probably it was. But Mike Saddler ... oh, I don't want to frighten you, Gil ... but Saddler's made Serena Jackson inform on you!"

Fred Stiles, the big storekeeper turned preacher, said firmly: "Not Serena. Why, she hid Gil. Why would Serena betray him?"

She told them. A moment later a horse came into the plaza at a jog. Stiles went to the door. Gil said: "Sis, get out. I've got a gun here. I'm ready for them."

But the horseman had reached the front of the church and his boots struck the steps. Stiles blocked the doorway. Looking past him, Fran saw that it was one of the two men who had been with Saddler at his cabin—the dark, leathery one named Wiley.

"Doyle's dyin'," Joe Wiley reported. "Can you come over to the hotel?"

"He's lying!" Fran exclaimed. "Doyle's already gone to Anvil."

Wiley's keen eyes found her behind the preacher. "No, ma'am, he only started. The bleeding started again and they had to bring him back. Doc Watkins don't give him long." Wiley came up the steps.

"Is that the truth?" Stiles asked uneasily.

Wiley silently raised his hand. Stiles glanced around at Fran. Wiley's hand clenched and he brought it down on the side of Stiles' neck. Stiles stumbled against the jamb, groaning. Wiley pounced like a cougar, driving two quick blows to his jaw. Sprawling, Stiles fell back into the church. Fran whirled to seize the rifle. An arm caught her from behind and the cowpuncher clasped her against him and stood against the wall. She felt a gun barrel in her side.

"That's how it's going to be, Becket," Joe Wiley said. "You, or both of you."

Fran tried to scream, but her throat had closed tight. She could see the barrel of a gun in the crawl hole above them.

Gil said: "Wiley, so help me I'll ..."

"Gil, I don't want a lot of talk," Saddler's man said. "Mike and Bill are waitin' in back with the horses. You ain't going to be hurt. Mike's made a deal with Jackson for a piece of Anvil. Jackson's promised you safe conduct to the railroad. A marshal will be waiting there to take you to Tucson. That's the best offer you're about to git, boy."

"They're lying, Gil!" Fran cried. "Stay where you are." Her fingers pried at Wiley's arm. It was as hard as the branch of a tree.

"Is ... is that on the level?" Gil asked Wiley.

"Jackson's word to Saddler. My word to you. But if you'd rather deal that way, I'll walk out right now. You and your sister can stand them off when they come. That's up to you, boy."

Fran could hear the rear door of the church open. "What am I going to do, Sis?" Gil groaned.

Wiley told him quietly: "Safe conduct. You won't be hearing that word again."

"He's right, Sis," Gil panted. "Only chance. I'm comin' down. Can I keep my gun?" he asked Wiley.

"Sure," Wiley said. "Why not?"

XX

Jim Jackson pulled up on some brushy high ground in the foot-hills, raising his gloved hand to halt the cowpunchers and loggers who rode with him. For over an hour they had followed the Defiance men into the foothills. Roth pulled up beside him. A quick, hard-ridden shortcut had put them on a ridge above the wagon road, so that the Defiance men were now approaching a point a few hundred yards below them, not far from Sheep Bridge, where Roth had held Cameron. Roth, his broken-nosed features grim, asked tightly: "Is he with them?"

"Don't know yet. We'll know in a minute, Red."

His rifle out, the rancher stared down through the small trees. He was beginning to suspect that the whole chase had been planned to draw them out of town.

Tom Doyle pulled alongside. Without looking at him, Jackson said: "How you making it, Tom?"

"OK, OK," Doyle repeated. He sounded strained and in trouble. The wound in his leg was deep. The doctor had done all he could for it, but Doyle should be in bed. It was Doyle's fault if he would rather help hang a man than get well.

"Yonder they come," Owen McCard breathed. And under his breath he named the riders passing beneath, far down the slope.

Jackson pressed against the saddle swell. "Edwards," he said. "Briscoe. Was that …?" Excited, thinking he had seen Becket, he shot a glance at Doyle. But Doyle, who had the eye of a chicken hawk, shook his head.

"Just some farmer," he growled.

In Jackson, rage cried for release. Fighting Cameron was like roping a whirlwind. You never quite got him in your loop. He had made up his mind that if he spotted Becket with them, he would have his crew open up on the whole gang. Aiding and abetting— they knew the law on that.

The riders below tailed out, took the last short pitch to Sheep Bridge, and clattered across it. "He ain't with them," Doyle said.

Jackson and Roth looked at each other. "OK, Big Jim," Roth asked grimly, "what's next? How'd you like to cut those trees yourself?"

Jackson's head turned. "Owen," he said to McCard, "take the boys on. We've got to keep an eye on those fellows in case they decide to mop up on Red's camp. Red … Tom … we're going back. Go on!" he shouted to McCard. "Didn't you hear what I said?"

McCard spurred down the slope and the others went with him. In their dust, Jackson, Doyle, and Roth sat their horses.

"Since Becket isn't with them," Jackson said, "he's still in hiding. Or was, until Saddler flushed him."

"You've got a lot of confidence in that blockhead," Roth said.

Jackson snugged the fingers of his buckskin glove, squinting. "No, let's say I've got confidence in my understanding of my daughter."

The arrangement with Saddler was that, if he got Becket, he would bring him to the Anvil turnoff. Roth's thin-skinned, freckled face was pessimistic.

"When you write Santa Claus this year, Jackson," he said, "tell him you need a new timber contractor."

"If the old one had any guts," Jackson said, "he wouldn't be walking out. I'm going down and wait for Saddler. If he hasn't got Becket, then It's up to you what you do. Nobody will blame you. But if you walk out on me now, you'll leave with a couple of new fractures in that nose of yours."

Roth's quiet eyes considered him. He had a way of withholding speech while you wondered what he was thinking. Beyond him Jackson was conscious of the blue bulk of the mountains rising— that godlike pile of stone and timber on which his destiny was written. In him there was a terrible wish to sweep everything away that stood between him and those mountains. But Cameron stood between him and them; Roth stood there; Becket stood there. His patience snapped.

"Do what you damned well please," he said abruptly. He wheeled his horse. Doyle turned with him, and in a moment he heard Roth following.

The short winter afternoon was chilling. Down into the leathery brush thickets they rode on the flats where the big, square adobe posts, anvil-topped, marked his turnoff. At once Jackson knew someone was waiting there. He had seen the two horses in the brush, and, as he watched, a man stood up and gave them a hat signal.

"He's got him!" Tom Doyle said. "He's got him!" In savage exultation he quirted his pony.

"Wait a minute, Tom!" Jackson reached for his arm, but Doyle was riding down the slope. The rancher noticed that his trouser leg was dark with blood. Roth took off his Stetson and gave it a throw. It sailed into the air as the logger loped after Tom Doyle.

Saddler had tied Gil Becket's wrists and ankles with a rope. Becket slumped at the base of a gatepost, unshaven, thin faced, frightened. Doyle dismounted and stood over him, his boots set widely. But Roth rode in and made his horse shoulder Doyle out of the way. Doyle stumbled on his bad leg.

"Simmer down," Roth said. He gazed down at Becket. "He's my 'coon. So this is what a killer looks like."

Becket said: "I didn't kill that fellow, Roth. There was three of us firing at once."

"But maybe you were the lucky one," Roth said.

There was a rope on his saddle that he had carried since the hour Deke Howard had been killed. He slipped the saddle string that held it, smiling down at Becket. Becket's bound hands clenched.

Watching him, Jackson felt only contempt. Once he had pitied Becket and his kind—too weak, too poor to flog a living from this tough country. But the cold knife of catastrophe had sliced away all his compassion. Becket had done murder. Now Becket belonged to Roth. Let Roth settle what to do with him.

"Git the horses," Roth said to Saddler.

Doyle's trout-like eyes probed coldly at him. "What for? He can walk a quarter-mile to a tree, can't he?"

"Where do you come in on this deal?" Roth demanded. "I'm taking Becket to town. The proper place for a hanging is a hay barn."

Saddler stood by, smoking a cigarette to hide his tension. Jackson saw his guilt and anxiety as he drawled: "Becket's sister knows we've got him. Becket was hiding in the church. She got there before I did, and I had to bring her along. We better stick with our deal. Safe conduct, we said."

"Now, that was bright!" Jim Jackson declared. "Where is she? Why didn't you leave her?"

Saddler's hat lay on the ground and his heavy, Indian-black hair had fallen into a natural part down the middle. His thumbs were pressed under his cartridge belt.

"I had my boys take her to the shack over in your Hay Ranch pasture. They'll hold her there till somebody goes for them. I couldn't leave her in town because Cameron was still around."

Roth said again, "Get the horses," and Saddler turned, reluctant but silently consenting. Tom Doyle opened a long clasp knife. Becket's eyes flinched as the gunman squatted before him, favoring his leg. Doyle made a quick motion and slashed the rope that bound his ankles. "Git up!" he said, standing back.

"Wait a minute, Tom," Jackson ordered. "This is Red's party. If he wants Becket in Frontera, he'll have him there."

Doyle turned so fast, still holding the knife, that the rancher thought at first he was going to attack him.

"Get it through your heads," the gunman said, "that I ain't got another hour's ride in me! We'll stretch him right here!"

Saddler led the horses back. He mounted silently, looking as if he preferred to be left out of it. Suddenly Becket charged him. He raised his bound hands and clawed at the rancher's arm. The horse shied and Saddler was half dragged from the saddle. With the ends of his braided rawhide reins he slashed at Becket's face until he fell back.

"Damn you, Gil!" he panted. "Straighten out!"

"You promised me a trial!" Becket shouted.

"I know, but ..." Saddler's eyes, angry and desperate and ashamed, swerved to Jim Jackson's face. Jackson smiled and said nothing. After a moment Saddler reined his horse away and murmured something to Roth, who swung from his buckskin. He took the reins of the extra horse from Saddler. "Let's go, boy," he said cheerfully to Gil.

Gil stood against the adobes. Roth lounged a couple of strides away, swinging the free end of his rope and grinning. Watching them, Jackson had the feeling: *They're jumping on strings, and the strings are in my hand.*

Then suddenly Gil drove at Roth, hammered his tied fists into his face, and charged across him as the logger fell back. He sprinted across the road into the brush, running like a rabbit, lithe, small, changing direction every instant.

Roth got up quickly, trying to draw his revolver, but Tom Doyle shoved him off balance and stepped into the road, his Colt cocked. His blunt features burned with excitement as he took his bead. "Runs like a jack rabbit." He chuckled. "Dang' little fool runs like a jack rabbit."

The Colt bucked, jumped a foot as the gray fumes burst from the muzzle, and the resounding crash of the shot deafened them. Jackson watched Becket falter, heard him cry out. Then the slender figure recovered and staggered on, one arm hanging loose.

Doyle cocked and pulled the gun down with greater care, biting his lower lip as he squinted. The Colt leaped. Across the road Gil Becket stumbled and went down. Doyle turned his pleased grin on Jackson.

"Dang' little fool run just like a jack rabbit, didn't he?" He chuckled again.

Mike Saddler uttered a curse and spurred at Doyle, smashing his fist down at the gunman's head. "What about our deal?" he shouted.

Damned fool's gone crazy, Jackson thought. *Well, lunacy is as good a way as any to dodge guilt.* Doyle stumbled, but he held onto the gun, and for the first time Saddler seemed to see it. With a quick slash of his quirt he knocked it from Doyle's hand. Then he rowelled his horse into the road and plunged into the low brush thickets.

A cold stream of purpose leveled out in Jim Jackson. Watching Saddler's hunched figure crowding the horse, he jacked a shell under the firing pin. As he gathered the horseman in his sights, he wondered if Saddler had finally realized that it needed only one shot to cancel the contract he and Nate Croft had forced on him. Nate was no fighter. He would take his money back when Jackson was ready to give it to him, and keep his mouth shut.

Saddler could not run the horse hard because of the brush. Jackson settled on an opening in the yellow-green creosote tangles. Just as Saddler pushed his pony across it, the rancher squeezed off the shot. Then he heard Doyle yell: "Got 'im, Jackson!"

Red Roth said nasally: "Nah. Just winged 'im. Your 'coon's gonna get away."

Saddler, hatless now and clinging to the horn, disappeared into the thicker brush. As Jackson prepared to follow him, he told Roth: "Better come along, Red. He's *our* 'coon, not just mine. He's got a lot of stories to tell, ever he reaches Frontera."

So when they took the trail after Mike Saddler, to corner and finish him, Red Roth disgustedly went with them.

XXI

It was curious how you could seldom remember your first estimate of a person after you had known him a while. But Troy had known Fran so short a while that he could recall exactly what he had thought of the haughty young woman who had arrived in Frontera a few days ago. He had judged her a rather sweet girl who needed some experience. Well, she had had it now. Yet it had not touched the fineness in her. It had only eliminated the foolishness and shown people she could take the jolts and grow stronger. And after he kissed her last night, she had come in singing.

He thought about her while he ate lunch. Having collected the things he would need for the desert crossing, he was trying to ease himself out with some food and coffee. But his nerves kept tightening like green rawhide, and, when Aperance suddenly said, "Say, the Becket girl was looking for you." Troy dropped his fork.

"When was this?"

"Maybe an hour apast."

"Did she say if anything was wrong?"

"Nope. Said everything was OK."

Troy walked hurriedly to the hotel. Why would she be hunting him, if everything was all right? Behind his wicket, Ed Mattson told him she had gone out. "But she might have come in the back way," he added. "I'll see."

"Never mind, I'll go back."

But she did not answer his knock. He moved to Serena's room and heard her cross the floor when he rapped. The door opened, and, seeing him, she bit her lip and her eyes filled with tears. Troy took her hands.

"Serena ... what's the matter?"

She could not speak for a moment. "I told them where Gil was," she whispered at last.

Troy swallowed hard. "Why?"

"To save Dad. They'd have killed him if I hadn't told them." Brokenly she told about the deal between Saddler and her father. Troy leaned against the doorjamb and rubbed his neck with his palm.

"When did this happen?"

"About an hour ago." She tried to summon an excited confidence. "He'll be all right, Troy. They promised to get him safely to—"

"Where's his sister?"

"Is it his sister you're worried about, or Gil?" Serena asked quietly.

Suddenly, as he studied her, he knew she had done this to get back at Fran. Whether she knew it or not, that was what she had been doing. Without a word he walked down the hall to the alley. Serena closed the door and followed him.

"Wait, Troy! I'll go with you."

Troy turned angrily. "Stay here! Do you want to see a lynching? Maybe a shooting? And know you set it up?"

"There won't be a lynching," Serena insisted. "Mike Saddler promised me. Dad had already left town, and Saddler was going to take Gil straight to the railroad."

Troy ran into the livery barn. He found his horse and was girthing up when Serena called to the hostler: "Pete! Saddle my black horse. Please hurry!"

Troy rode out the door and entered the plaza from the side gate. The church looked empty and forgotten. But when he approached it, he saw the big, corpulent man with disheveled gray hair seated on the ground near the base of the steps. He dismounted and knelt quickly beside him.

"What's happened, Fred?"

Stiles' eyes only half focused on him. There was a purplish bruise below his ear and a scraped, bloody patch on his cheek.

"Oh ... Troy," he muttered.

"What happened, Fred? Did they get Gil?"

Stiles rubbed his ear, a fat old man trying to remember. "Somebody ... Joe Wiley. Wiley got him. Somebody told him. And Gil's sister ..."

"Did she come with them?"

"She came to warn us."

"Fred, think about this. Was she here when they came for him?"

"Had a gun," Stiles recalled. "I took it away from her."

Troy ran up the steps. He halted with one hand on the edge of the door, gazing into the church. At once he saw the carbine leaning against the wall. He started to turn back to ask Stiles which way he thought they had gone, but apparently Stiles had been slugged as soon as Wiley walked in. He ran back through the church, looking for the girl. They wouldn't try to take her, he thought in panic. They'd tie her up and leave her. He searched through Stiles' rooms, but she was not there. He went out the back door and saw where the horses had stood. Kneeling, he found the prints of a girl's boots, and he stood again and gazed toward the mountains.

They had taken them both.

He went back into the church, shaken. He took his carbine from the vestibule. When he reached the front steps, he saw Fred

Stiles shambling off toward the Mexican stores across the plaza. Serena sat her horse beside his. He shoved his gun into the boot.

"Troy, are they gone?"

"Of course. The girl, too."

"But why?"

"Because she'd tell someone before they got far enough away."

"I'm going with you," Serena said as he mounted. "I'll make Dad keep the bargain. They won't be hurt, either of them."

"How can you make him keep his bargain when Gil is probably already dead?" Troy asked.

As he rode, she stayed with him for a time, but a mile out of town she began to fall back. After a while he let his horse drop into a fast jog. They had an hour's start on him, and all he knew now, in the middle of the afternoon, was that he had miles to cover. But their tracks were plain enough. Five horses traveling fast and keeping away from the road.

He came to where the trail split at the first lift of the foothills. Three horses had gone right here; two had continued straight on. He knelt, studying the tracks. Saddler rode a big Morgan horse and one of the horses traveling straight ahead had left the deep, round prints of a heavy animal. Saddler probably would be the one to take Gil. He would deliver him to Jackson and have Joe Wiley and that little fox-faced cowpuncher of his hold Fran somewhere until it was safe to let her go.

How safe would it ever be? She would know all about a murder. There was no use, now, trying to help Gil—one man alone against Jackson's and Roth's outfits. And he could not catch up with his own men, for they would have scattered at last to throw Jackson off completely.

He took the right fork, riding with his gun cocked, ready for them but knowing he might never see any of them again. They might keep going, cut south to Mexico and release the girl somewhere, keep going themselves. No telling now what Saddler's deal with them was.

What did she ever do, he asked himself rebelliously, *that she should run into all this? What have I ever done that I should fall in love with her?* For now he saw Serena as a child, breaking down under the weight of her fears, and Fran as a woman, and he was more afraid for her than he had ever been for himself.

Presently he knew where the trail was taking him. Jackson's Hay Ranch pasture was this way and there was a small hut on it. Once Jackson had kept a Mexican family there, raising hay in some good bottomland, but after being flooded out a few times he had given up. It was away from the main trails and yet close. He was almost sure Wiley and Thorne would take her there. He hit the horse with his spurs and it arched its neck and scuffed into a tired lope.

Shadows had begun to pour down the foothills when he halted above a wide wash. The old hayfields below still showed plainly, cropped over by cattle but well-graded and margined by rusting barbed wire. The hut near the far bank was an adobe, one room square, with a parapet roof and a sooty chimney like a melting piloncillo of sugar. A yellowing cottonwood grew at one side of it, and a rusted plow and some old harness lay close by. He saw no horses. It was about 250 yards across the wash to the hut.

He put his pony down the bank, and at that instant he heard a horse whicker, and a girl scream. He jabbed the horse with the spurs and bent over its neck. He heard the bullet hit the bank beside him and then came the *bang* and the cascading echoes of the rifle. The first heart-compressing shock left him. He felt exhilarated. She was here. She was all right!

As the pony struck the flats, he saw a drift of gun smoke from the roof of the hut. Then his eye picked up a flash in the window of the hut. Ahead of him was the dry, cobbled wash of the stream. He could not run his horse over this, and he left the saddle and hit the sand, running, carbine in hand. He fell just as a shot went over him with a silken tear.

A dark head showed above the mud parapet of the shack. Troy

steadied and let his shot go. He saw dust fly as the bullet hit the crumbling adobe. A man rose in a crouch, ran to the back, and leaped to the ground. The horses were tied there, for Troy saw him reappear a few moments later on a paint horse and lunge up the bank into the brush.

That's Bill Thorne, he thought dryly. *Brave Bill Thorne*. But it was not. For a moment later a man ducked out the door of the house, paused to fire two fast shots, and, as he started around the corner, Troy took him in his sights and recognized Thorne's tough, wiry form. The carbine kicked against his shoulder. Thorne fell— either hit or playing 'possum. Troy rose and started for the cabin. He hit the streambed with its gray, washed boulders. Up on the flats behind the cabin, Joe Wiley had drawn rein. As he took aim, Troy dropped behind a rock. The shot fell short and wailed off across the wash. Wiley loped on.

Troy rose to a crouch, watching for Thorne. He saw him lying close to the line shack, both arms flung out. Suddenly Fran came from the doorway, left the cabin, and ran toward Troy. Troy went back to pick up the reins of his pony. Then he hurried to meet her.

She was crying. Her hair, shining and golden, had come unpinned and hung to her waist. It was soft on his hands as he caught and held her. He pressed his face into it and whispered to her, stroking her cheek and telling her it was all right.

After a time he picked her up and carried her back to the cabin. He saw that Thorne had not moved.

He laid the girl on the cot in the cabin. Then he went out and put his saddle on her horse, which was rested, and brought her saddle blanket and Bill Thorne's Colt into the cabin. He went to his knees beside the cot and covered her with the blanket. She stopped weeping and watched him silently. He bent and kissed her. Her arm went across his shoulders.

"Are you going to tell me what you told me last night?" she whispered. "That it's possible to love one girl and yet ..."

"It's possible," he said, "to love a girl and not know it. Why didn't you tell me that?"

"I wanted you to find out," she said. "Troy, dear, we've got to follow Gil."

"I know." He knew that when he left her he might not be coming back again, and he kissed her again before he left the cot. "Where were they taking him?" he asked her, standing near the door.

"To the road to Jackson's ranch. Saddler kept telling us Gil wouldn't be hurt. I think Gil believed it. But I can't."

"They might have kept the promise. Gil might have gotten away. And ... anyhow, that Colt's loaded and on safety. Pull the hammer clear back if you need to fire it."

"No, I'm coming with you!"

"You can't. I'll be traveling fast, and I don't know how far. Don't let anyone near the cabin."

"Troy, you're alone, and there may be several men with Saddler now!"

"There's going to be one more with him before long," Troy promised.

XXII

After Troy left her, Serena turned toward the ranch. She was frightened and indignant. *It was the only thing I could have done*, she told herself. *They'd have killed Father if I hadn't.*

She wondered why the prospect of her father's death did not disturb her terribly. She was more afraid that they would lynch Gil Becket, because that would make her a party to his death—at least in Troy's eyes. She knew that, if Gil escaped, Troy would come back to her. *That Becket girl*, she thought. *Just so much fluff.*

She had not given them the notes she held on the Defiance Mountains ranches yet. Those would be worth quite a bit. With all that money, she and Troy could go away from here. *I wish I'd told him that*, she thought anxiously.

And then she heard gunfire. She stopped the horse, listening. It came from the rough brush and gully area to the north. She was almost to the ranch road. Anxiously Serena bit her lip. *They wouldn't dare kill him!* she thought. She hurried on, planning to go straight to the ranch. But then she realized that Troy might be involved in it.

When she reached the big adobe gateposts, she hesitated. Then she followed the hoof marks leading northwest into the brush. Suddenly her horse reared. Serena gasped, clutching at the horn of the saddle. She struck the horse with her reins. It came down, trembling, as it backed from something in the brush. Then she saw it—Gil Becket's body, sprawled under a large screw bean mesquite. His hands had been digging at the soil when he died. Serena turned her head and ran her horse on into the thickets.

Her father had done this. Big Jim Jackson, to stay big, had murdered the settler.

Again she heard the sound of guns. They had murdered Gil Becket. Were they trying to kill Troy? Serena drew the small buggy rifle she carried. She pushed on through the mesquite. She felt the last pins pulling from her hair as it shook loose, heavy and black. Then, hearing a shout, she peered ahead as she rode. The brush thinned on a high crease of land, and she saw something below that shocked her.

A small canyon pressed into the hills here and dead-ended. Its walls were steep and brushy. A man was crouched on the canyon floor, pointing a rifle almost at her.

Between her and the lip of the canon she saw two men on foot—Tom Doyle and her father. Red Roth sat his buckskin horse near them. They were all gazing down at Saddler, who was only a couple of hundred feet away, but fifty feet below. Only Roth's rifle was in its boot.

Saddler was aiming upward. He fired. The bullet struck low and Tom Doyle rose quickly and snapped a shot back at him. Saddler crouched against a cutbank at the edge of the canyon. He was already wounded. Serena felt sick. It was like one of those Mexican games—pulling the head from a rooster buried in sand, driving lances into a chained bear.

"Dad!" she screamed.

Jim Jackson pivoted. His face was contorted—broad,

red-mustached, vicious. Seeing her, he shouted: "Serena, go back! You hear?"

Serena started down to them. The brushy edge of the canyon protected Jackson, Doyle, and Roth from Saddler's fire, and, when he fired, they could shoot through a gap while he cocked his gun. But Roth was not firing, and, as she halted, she thought he looked angry and disgusted.

"Let him go, for God's sake!" he said. "He gave us Becket, didn't he? So why all this?"

"Where's your sporting blood?" Doyle chuckled. Doyle's hat hung between his shoulder blades by its rawhide lanyard. She had never seen a man so drunk, so shining with lunacy and the urge to kill. "Miss Serena," he suggested easily, "you all git down. Nothing but wild shots in that feller's gun."

"Naturally, since he's wounded," Serena said indignantly. She dismounted, went up to her father, and tugged at his gun. Jackson bushed her away. She fell against Roth's horse. Roth curbed the animal, and then he snapped at the rancher: "You may be kidding yourself, Jackson, but you aren't kidding me. If you kill Saddler, you're top dog on Anvil again. I got Becket. That's all I wanted. It's your party from here on out. I never kill for business reasons."

Jackson gazed stonily at him. Saddler fired another wild shot that ricocheted off a stone. Turning swiftly, Jackson snapped his rifle to his shoulder and took aim on the man crouched below. Serena cried: "Dad, if you kill that man …!"

Jim Jackson stood, tall and steady, squinting down the barrel of his gun at the black-haired man in the canyon. The gun blasted. Tom Doyle turned quickly to Jackson.

"Got your buck, boss. He's down."

I was part of this, Serena thought numbly. *I helped them.*

Roth patted her shoulder and reined his horse around. He had drawn his carbine and the hammer was back. "I'm just a working man, Jackson," he said. "I don't figure the tree's been planted that's worth all this. Why don't you do your own logging?"

"Take it easy, Red," Jackson said sternly. "I gave you Becket, didn't I?"

"Yes, with Saddler's hide thrown in. Maybe I didn't give a damn for Saddler. But I don't care much for bear baitin's, either."

Jackson's hawk eyes were grim. "What's the real trouble, Red? More money? OK, I'll sweeten it."

Roth showed his tobacco-flecked teeth in a grimace. "I figure your trouble's just starting, Jackson. What about Troy Cameron? Man, there ain't enough money in the territory to reconcile me to being dead. Adios, boys. Take care, Miss Serena."

Jackson's hand pressed down the gun Doyle wanted to raise. Roth kept his gaze on them as he wheeled. "Ladies present, Tom," said Jackson ironically. He watched the dust drifting into the thickets where the logger was riding. But Serena, gazing north, was watching another dust cloud. Someone was riding up from Hay Ranch. Was it Troy? She walked back to her horse, but her father was at her side when she reached it.

"Where to, Papoose?"

"I don't know. I'm going away. Take your hand off me!" She pulled away, and Jackson's big hand dropped.

"All right, we'll go together." He gazed up at the mountains, then out over the desert, and his face was old and ironic. "This range … I don't know, Papoose. They've ruined it, I reckon. There's nothing much left, is there?"

"There's nothing left," she said. She was watching the rider working up through the folds of scrub timber and brush.

"We'll go to Mexico," Jackson said with warmth. "We've got the money Croft paid me. We've got those notes of yours. We can leave them for collection. And I can sell my equity in Anvil for something. With that kind of money I'll be as big there as I ever was here." He helped her mount.

"I don't know where I'll go, Dad," she told him, "but it won't be with you. They didn't spoil this country. You spoiled it. You whipped the grass out of the range. You spilled blood and tricked an old preacher to save what was left of Anvil. You've worked hard for whatever comes to you. But whatever it is, good or bad, I don't want to share it."

Jackson's face hardened. "All right, Serena. I've learned to do without 'most everything in my time. I can do without a daughter who never did understand what I wanted. You know," he remarked thoughtfully, "you'd better not count on those notes being worth much, if you were figuring to finance an elopement with Cameron with them."

"What do you mean?"

"Why, there's no telling what will happen now," he replied, frowning down at the body of Mike Saddler. "I'm just superstitious enough to think a good thing for me would be to travel fast."

"What's that got to do with the notes?"

Jackson took a match from his hatband and examined it. "I mean that I don't want to be bothered with people sharpshooting at me after I take off. So I'm going to give them something to do for a few days." He struck the match with his thumbnail. As it flared up, he said: "A mortgage on timber lands wouldn't be worth much if the timber burned, would it?"

He scanned the long sweep of mountains. Serena clenched the reins. She looked at his profile for an instant, seeing the hardness of his chin and the heavy brow line, the battering-ram determination and ruthlessness in his face.

"You'd do it, wouldn't you?" she marveled.

"Stick around and see. They say you can't take it with you … but I'll bet I don't leave much, either."

"Horsebacker comin'," Doyle growled.

Jackson regarded the rider working up through the brush. "Looks like that Basco cowpuncher of Saddler's." He glanced down at Saddler's body. "Maybe a good idea would be to let him think

Saddler's still alive. We could cut him off and say Saddler's holding Becket at the ranch."

Doyle shrugged. "There's another way to handle him, ain't there?"

"I'm thinking we can use his gun," Jackson replied.

Serena understood. If Wiley were coming in such a hurry, Troy might be behind him. As if he had read her thoughts, Jackson looked fully into her face as he passed.

"Papoose, you don't think I'm fool enough to leave a trained man hunter on my back trail? Not when I can put him out of action first."

She did not reply. But as soon as they rode away, heading on a detour around the high cleft of the canyon to meet Joe Wiley, she loped into the brush on a game trail that led toward Hay Ranch.

XXIII

Now and then, stopping to listen, Troy caught the sounds of Wiley's horse breaking through the mesquite thickets. Once he caught a glimpse of him crossing an open space. Wiley had about a quarter mile lead. He wondered how deep Joe Wiley's craft ran. Would he lead him to where they were holding Gil, or would he know that was what Troy wanted him to do, and take him on a long swing into the hills?

He checked his horse, hearing shots. He had grown pessimistic about Gil's chances. Yet he had to keep pushing after Gil as if he were alive and there were a way to save him. Like a lost soldier, he thought yearningly of his companions riding high in the Defiances.

The shots were too distant to have come from Wiley's gun. Wiley was moving on. Troy followed quickly. The foothills were ragged with mesquite and creosote brush, the ground bare at intervals, then so densely thicketed that the starved soil supported no graze at all, and a rider must shield his face with his arm as he passed.

For a quarter of an hour he worked up along the tilted hillside.

All at once as he came to the crest of a knoll he saw three riders lined up on a ridge not far ahead. Between Troy and the horsemen lay matted thickets of tornillo. As though they had been waiting for him to come in view, one of the riders gave him a hat signal and his voice came far off and deep.

"Cameron! Wait there!"

He knew Jackson's voice. And that was Wiley beside him.

"I've got Becket!" Jim Jackson shouted. "Do you want to trade for him?"

"Where is he?" Troy called back.

"Will you trade?"

Either Gil was dead or he had escaped. For Jackson could not afford to trade him off. He was the one thing Jackson could not trade, because Gil Becket belonged to Red Roth.

"If you can show him to me," he agreed, "I'll make a trade."

Jackson spoke to the men with him and they reined away into the thickets. Jackson stayed on the ridge. "I'll show him to you in five minutes. He'll be right here beside me."

Troy remained there on the knoll in the mesquite. *What's his game?* he asked himself. *He won't trade, so what's to gain by pretending he will?* Was Jackson trying to slow him down while they hauled Gil off somewhere?

He waited, keeping his eye on Jackson. Then his pony quivered and turned its head. Birds and rodents were making small sounds in the brush, but the horse had spooked at something else. At last he heard it. A horse was moving up from the left, down the hill. In a short time he heard the other horse above him. Then he realized that Jackson was holding his attention while Wiley and the second rider closed in.

Troy set the butt of his rifle against his shoulder and waited. But the rider below him was coming too rapidly for a cautious man like Wiley. Through a break in the thicket he saw a flash of black horsehide and a sparkle of harness trim. He set himself. A moment later the horse broke into the open. He went slack with relief. It was Serena.

Seeing him, she rode hurriedly to his side. Her black hair was shining and loose, and in the early dusk her face was pale. "Troy, it's an ambush!" she cried.

"I'd about decided that," Troy said, "How many men does he have with him?"

"Just Doyle and Joe Wiley. Roth has quit him."

He listened to the brush. Wiley was not the only one moving in. Another rider was working up on almost the line Serena had followed.

"Quit him?" Troy said. "Why? He's got Gil, hasn't he?"

She shook her head. "No one has Gil, now."

Across the mesquite he gazed at Jackson. Now at last he knew the man he had been fighting. *If I'd known him before*, he thought, *if I'd known there's no line he draws, we could have had our showdown early.* But Gil was gone. A logger had been killed. Jackson had pulled them into a losing war because they gave him credit for ethics.

"Who killed him?" he asked.

"Dad and the others. I found his body near our road. Then I came on and found them finishing Mike Saddler. But Roth quit because he realized Saddler was being murdered for business reasons."

The rider up the hill was behind them now. He was coming quietly and steadily. In his mind Troy could see Joe Wiley's oaken features peering through the brush. He and Jackson and Doyle had him in the shrinking center of a triangle.

Serena was explaining the deal Croft and Saddler had forced on her father. "But now you're the only one left that he's afraid of. He's getting out, but he knows you'd lead the hunt for him, where the others would probably lose heart."

Listening to the riders drawing closer, he had the picture in his mind. It was too late now to break out without a fight. And now he had Serena to worry about, too. "The safest place for you," he said quickly, "is right here. If you're moving, they might fire at you by accident. Wiley's back of us now, and Doyle's down the slope."

"Troy, I won't leave you. We'll go together."

Wiley was closing in, stopping every few yards to study, then moving on again. "If you're with me," Troy said, "you'll be hurt. Stay here and they won't bother you."

He touched the horse with his spurs, but she clutched his arm, moving with him. "Troy, I'm not Big Jim's girl any more. Don't you know that? I'm just Serena. Doesn't that mean anything to you?"

He looked at her plainly. She would always be Big Jim's girl, although she might not know it. She would always trade for the quick escape, even when a man's life was the commodity.

"I don't know," he said. "It used to mean everything. But whatever we had, it went with Gil."

Her face changed. She could still be haughty. "No, it went with his sister," she said. "She's waiting for you, isn't she?"

"If I get back."

"Even though I'm the one who took the risk to help you. Troy, are you blind? Do you think a man with your ambition can ever be happy with a little seamstress?"

He smiled. *How little she ever knew me*, he thought. If she believed the distinction of having Big Jim's daughter on his arm had been part of his love for her, she had never known him at all. He said quietly: "A seamstress should be just right for me. The only real ambition I have is to stay out of fights for the rest of my life."

He moved her hand from his arm and spurred ahead. This time she did not follow. The brush came between them. He heard Doyle's and Wiley's horses break into a run.

Doyle was ahead of him on the left, his horse lunging up the slope to intercept him as he rode toward Jim Jackson. He saw Jackson leave the ridge and rowel his horse over to Troy's right. That closed the ring. The only strategy worth anything was strategy of the club: to go in fighting.

He chose Doyle. Doyle had been in the saddle all day on a bad leg and should be the weakest link. Clouds of gnats swarmed through the oppressively fragrant brush. About fifty yards away, Doyle slowed down. Troy slipped from the saddle. He moved along an aisle in the brush until he was fifty feet from his pony. There he stopped.

Again Doyle was in motion. He would move on, check his horse, and again advance. Troy brought the rifle up. The footfalls of the gunman's horse were very close. Then he saw Doyle come through a thicket. Without warning, Doyle's gun blasted. Troy's pony reared, terrified. Doyle fired again and charged in at the horse half seen by him. The horse swerved and went buck jumping into the brush. Doyle dropped his Colt and pulled his saddle gun. He looked taut and sick as he searched for Troy. Blond stubble spiked his jaws, thorns had scratched his face, and his trouser leg was black with drying blood. He looked crazy with anger, but the slitted gunfighter's eyes saw Troy's empty saddle and he swiveled abruptly. Across the reddish ground they stared at each other, and in the action of turning Doyle slapped his cheek against the stock of the carbine and pulled the trigger.

He was fast as a cat, but this was gambler's speed, the speed of a man desperately trying to catch up. The shot split a branch beside Troy's head. The sound of it was shattering. Doyle whipped the loading piece down, slammed it back, and fired again. Between them the smoke thickened. Troy fired, feeling cool and sure, and then he watched. Doyle dropped his gun. His pony began pitching, and he fell. He raised his head and saw Troy, and, swearing, he crawled after his gun. Troy put the second shot at the base of his neck. Tom Doyle's body eased down on the earth as the stiffness and restless urging went out of him.

Then Troy heard them coming—Wiley from the rear, Jackson driving in hard from the right. He paused to reload and started after his pony. He whistled, but could not hear it. Cutting right, he tried to spot Doyle's horse. It was gone. He turned, hearing Jim Jackson's big horse traveling up the slope. Then he heard Jackson shout in a voice like a shotgun: "Wiley! He's afoot! Yonder's his horse. This way!"

Wiley called something back. He sounded very close. Desperately Troy cast about for cover. The mesquite trees, shade starved and spindly, were the only shelter in sight. Troy stood behind one. Jackson and the cowboy were trying to time it to strike him at once. They were coming fast, sure of their man. Troy knelt by the tree. He held his saddle gun.

Then a woman screamed. The sound was short and clear and delivered the way only a woman could do it—with an edge that sliced your nerves like a fleshing knife. It stopped Jackson, up on the slope. It stopped Wiley. Wiley said something. Then a small-bore rifle cracked, and Wiley cried out. In the brush it was utterly silent. Jackson halted. Troy stared toward the thicket where he had left Serena. Then he understood. With that foolish little .25-caliber buggy rifle of hers, Serena had stopped Wiley! As Jackson came in view, he turned to make a smaller target. Jackson had lost his hat, and branches had ripped his face, but he looked enormous in the saddle. Huge and dangerous, like a grizzly flushed by a cowboy who was after a steer. He came with the menacing force of rage and physical power, a man who had just been beaten at something for the first time in his life. Troy waited for his first angry, wild shot, but finally realized Jackson was playing the same game—holding the single shot that would settle everything.

With a snap, the rancher checked his horse. He took aim. Troy fired, but in the same moment he felt the concussion of Jackson's gun. Smoke roiled between them. Troy leaned back against the mesquite as he cocked the rifle. He did not think he had hit Jackson. Jackson was still in the saddle. He was levering another bullet into the breech, grinning the way he had grinned that day they had fought in the street. He tilted his head to aim, taking it easy, doing it right.

Troy's shot went off. He rocked with the recoil.

Jackson's body convulsed. He reeled, clutching at the saddle horn. He let his saddle gun fall. Blood streaked his face. His face darkened with effort, and then he drew his Colt, spurring the horse on. But he rode like a drunken man. The horse bucked twice and buried its head, and Jackson went over the swell. His head and shoulder took the shock as he landed. He rolled and sprawled on his back. The Colt was still in his hand. He lay about fifteen feet from Troy, his eyes open, his jaw loose.

It was silent in the thickets. Troy thought of Serena. He called to her, and after a moment she called back. "All right?" he shouted.

"Yes! Are you hurt, Troy?"

"No, but I've got a long walk ahead of me! I've lost my horse!"

"I'll bring Wiley's!" Serena called back.

He walked up the slope until he met her in a clearing, leading a horse. She was white and dry eyed. He took the reins. When he moved to place his saddle gun in Wiley's empty sheath, he saw the blood on the saddle.

"Wiley didn't think I counted," she said stiffly. "So he rode right past me. I … I did what I had to."

Troy swung up. He did not want to look at her. There was a debt he could not pay, and there were no gentle words left to explain it.

"I'll ride to the ranch with you," he told her. "You'll be all right there."

After they had ridden a short distance she said: "You don't need to ride with me. I'm all right. I showed that, didn't I?"

"I could say thanks," he said, "but it wouldn't be a start."

"Apparently," she said, "it will have to do." She checked her horse and looked at him with a queer intensity. "Tell your friends not to worry about their notes. They can pay as they're able."

"That's fine of you," he said. "But what will you do about the ranch?"

"Perhaps I can save something. I have some time to sell it. I might go to Mexico. Money goes a long way there. I could buy a ranch as big as Anvil."

Her face brightened as she saw herself in the new role that was merely the old one rewritten. Not as Big Jim's girl, but as *la patrona*, the boss lady. Quickly, then, she rode away.

Troy turned his horse to return to Hay Ranch.

The sun was setting, its wine and gold flowing down from the crest of the Defiances. It was good to ride alone in the coolness and peace, riding from something ugly to something beautiful. He thought of all the things he wanted to do. But the thing he wanted most was to get back to Fran, and presently he slackened the reins and let the horse rock into a long, reaching lope.

THE END

ABOUT THE AUTHOR

Frank Bonham, in a career that spanned five decades, achieved excellence as a noted author of young adult fiction and detective and mystery fiction, as well as making significant contributions to Western fiction. By 1941 his fiction was already headlining Street and Smith's *Western Story*, and by the end of the decade his Western novels were being serialized in the *Saturday Evening Post*. His first Western, *Lost Stage Valley* (1948), was purchased as the basis for the motion picture, *Stage to Tucson* (Columbia, 1951) with Rod Cameron as Grif Holbrook and Sally Eilers as Annie Benson. "I have tried to avoid," Bonham once confessed, "the conventional cowboy story, but I think it was probably a mistake. That is like trying to avoid crime in writing a mystery book. I just happened to be more interested in stagecoaching, mining, railroading ..." Yet, notwithstanding, it is precisely the interesting—and by comparison with the majority of Western novels—exotic backgrounds of Bonham's novels that give them an added dimension. He was highly knowledgeable in the technical aspects of transportation and communication in the 19th-Century American West. In introducing these backgrounds into his narratives, especially when combined with his firm grasp of idiomatic Spanish spoken by many of his Mexican characters, his stories and novels are elevated to a higher plane in which the historical sense of the period is always very much in the forefront. This historical aspect of his Western fiction early drew accolades from reviewers so that on one occasion the *Long Beach Press Telegram* predicted that "when the time comes to find an author who can best fill the gap in Western fiction left by Ernest Haycox, it may be that Frank Bonham will serve well." Among his best Western novels are *Snaketrack* (1952), *Night Raid* (1954), *The Feud at Spanish Ford* (1954), and *Last Stage West* (1959).

ABOUT THE EDITOR

Bill Pronzini was born in Petaluma, California. His earliest Western fiction was published under his own name and a variety of pseudonyms in *Zane Grey Western Magazine*. Among his most notable Western novels are *The Last Days of Horse-Shy Halloran* (1987) and *Firewind* (1989). He is also the editor of numerous Western story collections, including *Under the Burning Sun: Western Stories* (Five Star Westerns, 1997) by H. A. DeRosso, *Renegade River: Western Stories* (Five Star Westerns, 1998) by Giff Cheshire, and *Tracks in the Sand* by H. A. DeRosso (Five Star Westerns, 2001). His own Western story collection, *All the Long Years* (Five Star Westerns, 2001), was followed by *Burgade's Crossing* (Five Star Westerns, 2003), *Quincannon's Game* (Five Star Westerns, 2005), and *Coyote and Quarter-Moon* (Five Star Westerns, 2006). He also wrote *Crucifixion River* with Marcia Muller. Its original title novella won a Spur Award from the Western Writers of America for the best short fiction of 2007.